ENEMY MATCH

NANCY DREW MYSTERY STORIES®

ENEMY MATCH

by
Carolyn Keene

Illustrated by
Paul Frame

WANDERER BOOKS

Published by Simon & Schuster, Inc., New York

Published by WANDERER BOOKS
A Division of Simon & Schuster, Inc.
Simon & Schuster Building
1230 Avenue of the Americas
New York, New York 10020

Manufactured in the United States of America
10 9 8 7 6 5 4 3 2

NANCY DREW and NANCY DREW MYSTERY STORIES
are trademarks of Stratemeyer Syndicate,
registered in the United States Patent
and Trademark Office

WANDERER and colophon are registered trademarks of
Simon & Schuster, Inc.

Library of Congress Cataloging in Publication Data

Keene, Carolyn.
Enemy match.

(Nancy Drew mystery stories ; #73)
Summary: Nancy Drew tries to stop threats against her friend, a
professional tennis player, while also searching for the girl's father
and evidence which will prove he didn't commit a crime for which
he's been convicted. [1. Mystery and detective stories] I. Frame,
Paul, 1913–   ill. II. Title. III. Series: Keene, Carolyn.
Nancy Drew mystery stories ; #73.
PZ7.K23Nan no. 73   [Fic]   83-19836
ISBN 0-671-49736-7
ISBN 0-671-49735-9 (pbk.)

CONTENTS

1

A Call for Help

Nancy Drew's blue eyes filled with tears as she read the final words of the letter written to her by her former schoolmate, Nina Ford.

> *Please help me, Nancy. I don't know where else to turn. I must find out what happened to my dad and clear his name.*

She put the letter down and tried to turn away so that Hannah could not see that she was upset. Hannah peered at Nancy over her glasses. "What is it? Is something wrong, dear?"

The woman had been the Drews' house-keeper ever since Nancy's mother had died, and had taken care of Nancy since she was a baby.

Nancy forced a smile. "Oh, it's just an old friend who's having a problem and wants me to help."

"Must be something serious, from the look on your pretty face."

The girl detective nodded and then, impulsively, hugged the housekeeper. "Oh, Hannah, you're such a flatterer. But I love you."

Hannah hugged her in return. Then she took Nancy by both arms and held her at a distance. "Well, are you going to take the case, even though the River Heights Bicentennial is coming up so soon?"

Nancy grinned. "Of course. I have no choice. Besides, the bicentennial is more than a week away. When an old friend is in trouble, I can't turn her down. *You* taught me that, Hannah."

Suddenly a new voice broke in. "Take what case? Oh, don't tell me you're planing to go off on another adventure this week of all weeks!" The words came tumbling out of Bess Marvin, Nancy's pretty blond friend, who had burst through the front door and into the kitchen, obviously excited.

Rumpling her hair with both hands, she flopped into a comfortable chair, exhaling dramatically. "What a morning I've had. I worked my fingers to the bone down at the bicentennial office. Oh, Nancy, you should see your dress! It's white, and it must have fifty thousand yards of satin and lace. It's gorgeous! You're going to be the most beautiful queen of this century!"

Both Nancy and Hannah smiled at the girl's typical display of enthusiasm. Bess and her cousin, George Fayne, were two of Nancy's best friends. George, however, was away for the summer visiting her grandparents in California.

As Bess noticed the somewhat mixed emotions on Nancy's face, she suddenly remembered the conversation she had overheard when she rushed in.

"Oh, oh," said Bess. "We're in trouble, aren't we? You're taking on another case, right?"

Nancy added.

"With only a little more than a week before being crowned queen of the bicentennial celebration? I can't believe it! Do you realize what will happen if you don't show up?"

"Of course I do. Kimberly van Rensselaer will take my place."

"But she's the snootiest, snobbiest, most arrogant girl who ever lived in River Heights."

"Oh, Bess. I know a lot of people feel the

same way, but you have to admit she *is* beautiful. Besides, she was elected first runner-up, fair and square."

Bess put her hands over her ears. "Just the thought of it makes me ill," she said. She pulled Nancy into the living room, sat her down on the sofa, and continued. "Look, I don't care if you *are* a detective. What mystery could be so important that you would give up being queen of the River Heights Bicentennial?"

Instead of replying, Nancy handed Bess the letter, written on pale blue stationery, that she had received that morning. "Read that, Bess, and tell me what you would do."

Bess read it aloud.

> *"Dear Nancy,*
>
> *"It's been so long since I've been in touch with you, but so much has happened over the past year that I've been in a daze.*
>
> *"First, my dad was accused of committing mail fraud about a year ago. I know he's innocent, Nancy, but he couldn't prove it. He was sentenced to five years in jail!*
>
> *"Then, something even worse happened. When they were taking him to*

the penitentiary, the police car in which he was riding was swept away in a flood on the New Brighton River. He was never found.

"I'm now living with Mr. and Mrs. Calisher. Mr. Calisher was Dad's business partner. They have been very sweet to me, but they can't help me with this problem. I'll explain when I see you. Please meet me at Benton's coffee shop in New Brighton at noon on Tuesday.

"I'm really desperate. Please help me, Nancy. I don't know where else to turn. I must find out what happened to my dad and clear his name.

> *Affectionately,*
> *Nina"*

Bess looked up, her face stricken. "How terrible!" she said. "And here I thought Nina was on top of the world. She's considered to be one of the best tennis players around. As a matter of fact, my father was saying just the other day that she might be able to go on to be a national champion."

The two girls reminisced about Nina and

11

what good friends they had all been in school. Then, when she was fourteen, Nina's mother had died and her father moved his business to New Brighton. The girls had lost touch with each other except for the reports in the sports pages about Nina's success as a tennis player.

They recalled, too, how Mr. Ford had been a great favorite of the neighborhood children. He had amused them with his tennis clown act and trick shots on so many quiet summer afternoons. Having been a tournament player himself, he was Nina's coach when she started.

Then the girls' conversation lagged and they found themselves staring into space until Nancy finally broke the spell.

"Well," Nancy said and got up, "there's no use putting off the agony any longer."

"You're not going to New Brighton, are you?" Bess asked. "Nina said she'd meet you *tomorrow.*"

"I'm going down to the bicentennial office to make my excuses."

"Wait," Bess begged, tugging at Nancy's sleeve, as both girls walked outside. "Don't be too hasty. The bicentennial isn't until the fifteenth. Maybe you can finish the case and get back from New Brighton by the fourteenth, just in time for rehearsal. Oh, Nancy, don't just cancel out. New Brighton isn't that far, and you know how great you are under pressure!"

Nancy took in a deep breath and laughed at her friend's pleas. "All right, Bess, but I have to go down to the festival office and explain the situation."

"Hello, everybody." It was Carson Drew striding up the path. Mr. Drew, a lawyer, was his usual affable self. "Anything happening around here?"

"Of course," said Nancy, as he and the girls sat down on the porch for a moment. "I just received a sad letter from Nina Ford. She told me her dad had been convicted of mail fraud and that on the way to prison he was swept away in a flood on the New Brighton River. Dad, did you know about that?"

Carson Drew stretched his long legs and tapped out his pipe thoughtfully.

"Nancy, I'm sorry. I think that occurred while you were out of town. When you got back, so many things happened, I guess I never did tell you.

"By the time I found out about the trial and John's disappearance it was too late for me to provide any legal assistance. I do wish he had called me, but his firm employed their own lawyer."

13

"Dad, would you represent Mr. Ford if I find him and turn up evidence?"

"Absolutely," her father said. "Poor Nina, she's virtually an orphan now. Who is she living with? I know the Fords had no close relatives."

"She's staying with the Calishers. You know, Mr. Calisher was Mr. Ford's business partner."

Mr. Drew frowned and looked down. He started to speak and then he stopped.

"What is it, Dad?"

"Oh, nothing. It's just that Calisher was kind of an odd duck. Highly emotional type. Anyway, if you take the case, you'll miss out on the bicentennial, won't you?"

"Probably," Nancy said. "I don't see how I can be in two places at once."

"Hmm," Carson Drew said, "well, that's disappointing. Probably more so for me than for you, Nancy. I'm very proud my daughter was named queen of the River Heights Bicentennial. I guess Kimberly will fill in for you."

Bess frowned. "I may throw myself under her float in the middle of the parade just to protest the whole thing."

"Now, Bess, maybe Nancy can do both jobs. Anyway, a friend is worth more than a crown. And you shouldn't be too hard on Kimberly. She can't help the fact she was born both rich and pretty. Think how hard it must be for her to make friends with everybody envying her."

"Remember the Christmas dance?" Bess asked Nancy. "She wasn't satisfied to have one date. She wanted to dance with every boy on the floor."

Nancy laughed. "I think she did, too."

"She'll grow out of it," Nancy's father said with a twinkle. "I went to school with her dad, you know. He was rather arrogant himself and hard to get along with when he was young. But he's mellowed with time. He even lets me tee off first when we play golf."

The laughter was interrupted by the ring of the telephone. Hannah appeared at the door.

"Nancy, it's your friend Nina."

Mr. Drew and the two girls returned to the living room where Nancy took the phone.

"Nina! Hello! Oh yes, I have your letter right here. I'm just so sorry about everything that's happened."

Nina's voice came through strained and halting. "Nancy, can you meet me tomorrow?"

"Of course."

"Oh, thank you," Nina began to sob. "I need you more than ever now, Nancy. Someone is threatening me!"

2

A Mysterious Car

Nancy gasped at Nina's words. "What do you mean you're being threatened? Have you been getting calls or letters?"

Carson Drew and Bess were electrified by Nancy's half of the conversation. Bess shifted from one foot to the other, mouthing the question, "What's happening?"

But Nina cut the conversation short. "I can't talk now. Please meet me and I'll tell you everything. And please, don't try to call me here at the Calishers. Good-bye, Nancy."

"Wait," Nancy cried, but too late. Nina Ford had hung up.

Nancy replaced the phone and told her father and Bess how frightened Nina had been. "That settles it," the young detective concluded.

"Dad, Bess and I are going now to tell the bicentennial people. I'm leaving for New Brighton tomorrow."

The moment Nancy and Bess arrived at the festival office a stout, friendly woman greeted them. "Nancy, you must try on your gown."

"I will," the girl said hesitantly, "but I'm really here to give you some news that might change things."

Mrs. Milton was only half listening as she held out the dress. She and Bess oohed and ahed as they slipped the garment over Nancy's head and smoothed the great clouds of white material. Nancy could not help but smile as she admired the lovely dress, which was fashioned after an eighteenth-century ballgown.

But while she changed back into her street clothes, she told Mrs. Milton that she had to go out of town.

The woman's face fell, for Nancy was one of her favorites. "Not be the queen?" she asked. "Nancy, what in the world would prevent you?"

"Yes, Nancy," a sarcastically sweet voice purred from behind a dressing room curtain. "What could make the great Nancy Drew miss such an honor?"

The curtain parted and a striking, black-haired girl with almond-shaped brown eyes appeared dressed in a flowing blue gown.

"Kimberly," groaned Bess. The girl turned and leveled a superior look.

"Hello, Kimberly," Nancy said, "you look lovely."

"Thank you, Nancy. You are *so* gracious," Kimberly said. She paced back and forth, admiring herself in the full-length mirror.

"Excuse me, Kimberly," Mrs. Milton said frostily, "but I believe you interrupted Nancy."

"*Oh,* so I did. I apologize. Do go on, Nancy," Kimberly said airily.

Bess ground her teeth as Nancy, taking a deep breath, continued, "I have just had a call about an urgent matter and I might not be available for rehearsal on the fourteenth. If I let you know by the evening of the thirteenth, will that be time enough?"

"Well, yes," Mrs. Milton said in disappointment. "But I'm terribly distressed to think you might not be our queen." She looked at Kimberly. "We all feel that way, don't we?"

"Crushed," the girl said, lifting one shoulder and gazing over it at Nancy. "I'm simply crushed. But, of course, your business must come first."

"It's not business," Bess flared. "Nancy has to help a friend who's in trouble. That's something you wouldn't understand!"

"Now, now!" Mrs. Milton said sharply. "No more of that."

With a haughty sweep, Kimberly disappeared behind the curtain again. Bess murmured an apology to Mrs. Milton and excused herself to do some shopping, telling Nancy she would get home on her own.

After settling a few details, Nancy said good-bye to Mrs. Milton and walked back to the parking lot, where she had left her car.

She was about to open the door when she was startled by a voice from the back seat.

"Hi, Nancy. Boy, you were gone a long time."

Nancy saw a smiling face with big, green eyes, freckles, and a mop of bright red hair. It belonged to a young girl, about thirteen or fourteen years old. She was barefoot and wore faded overalls and a rough boy's shirt.

"I'm Midge Watson. And I've been waiting for you because I'm your new assistant!"

Nancy's mouth dropped open. "What!"

"You do need an assistant, Nancy. *All* great detectives have assistants. Look at Sherlock Holmes. He had Dr. Watson. Well, my name is Watson, too." The girl giggled.

Nancy recovered from her surprise and leaned forward with both hands on the car door. "Well, Miss Watson, I'm afraid you've come to the wrong detective. I don't need an assistant and I certainly didn't advertise for one."

"Aw, Nancy."

"That's final," Nancy said. She motioned the girl out of the back seat, got in the car and turned the key. Then she looked at the sad little face. "Where do you live, Midge?"

"On the north side."

"That's a long way from here. How did you get downtown?"

"Hitched a ride on the back of a truck."

Nancy shook her head in disapproval. "You're kidding!"

"Well, I couldn't afford the bus fare. I have an old secondhand bike that Morton the mechanic gave me, but it's broken—so what could I do?"

"I suppose you were planning to hitch a ride back the same way."

"Guess so."

"Does your mother know you travel like this?" Nancy asked.

"My mom died."

"Oh, I see. I'm sorry, Midge. And your father?"

"Dad's at home."

"Get in," Nancy said. "I'll take you there."

Midge giggled cheerfully and jumped in the front seat. "Thanks, Nancy," she said.

"You're welcome."

As they drove away, Midge renewed her

pleas. "Are you sure you couldn't use me? I'm awfully good."

"Obviously, you have some interesting qualities," Nancy said. "You're confident . . . you have a nice smile . . . you speak well. . . ."

"Does that mean if I talk some more, you may say yes?"

Nancy sighed. "I suppose I can't stop you from talking."

"Okay," Midge bubbled. "In the first place, I can lick almost anybody on the north side who's anywhere *near* my height and weight. I mean I can lick girls, boys, cats, dogs, even mountain lions."

Nancy laughed in spite of her determination not to.

"Not only that," Midge continued, feeling encouraged, "I can track and trail anything that walks, crawls, runs, or rolls. I'd have won a merit badge for tracking, but they kicked me out of the Girl Scouts."

"Why?"

"For fighting."

"For fighting? That's no way to settle anything, Midge. It only works against you."

Her companion lowered her eyes as Nancy continued. "You know, most detective work depends on sensitivity. You need the ability to observe things other people miss. You must put together clues that often seem to have no connection. You'd be surprised how often a polite manner succeeds when a rude one fails—especially since it is so important in this job to get along with people, such as witnesses and the police, and—"

"Hmm, I see," Midge said suddenly. "That's one of the reasons I want to be your assistant—so you can teach me to act more polite!"

Nancy glanced at the girl and grinned. "Now tell me more about your detective qualities."

"Well, I can drive a car."

"What? But you can't be more than thirteen."

"I'm fourteen. Almost fifteen," Midge said.

"Still, you're not allowed to drive a car in this state until you're sixteen."

The girl pouted. "Well, if you won't let me drive your car, I could be your mechanic. I can fix things. I know how to change tires, take care of the battery, and I can start a car without a key."

"That's what thieves do."

"I never stole anything in my whole life," Midge replied indignantly.

"I certainly didn't mean to suggest that. But where did you learn such things?"

"My friend Morton the mechanic showed me. Besides, people steal cars in my neighborhood, and I watch them sometimes. I've helped the police catch thieves lots of times."

"Do you go to school?" Nancy asked.

"Sure, but school's out for the summer. So I could work for you full-time for two months. I've got a suitcase. I could travel. I wouldn't even expect any composition at first."

"Compensation," Nancy corrected. Then she stopped. "Did you mean to say salary?"

Midge nodded a bit anxiously. "Just kind of an allowance?"

"Oh, I see."

"You know, for taxis when I have to trail suspects. Or when I have to bribe somebody."

Nancy shook her head. "Good detectives don't have to do that. My father taught me that witnesses who can be bribed usually aren't reliable."

"Okay, I won't bribe anyone. But what do you say, Nancy? Couldn't I help you?"

"I'll think about it," Nancy said.

"Oh, then you'll say yes."

"I said, I'll *think* about it."

"That's good enough for me. Now I'm going to give you my first tip. A green Chevy, four doors, with dark-tinted windows and no license plate in front, has been following us all this time!"

3

Nina's Story

Startled by Midge's revelation, Nancy checked the rear-view mirror. "Why, I didn't even notice that car. I should have. A detective has to be alert and not let herself be distracted by anything."

"Like me, huh?" Midge demanded.

Nancy smiled. "No fair, Midge."

When she pulled up to Midge's trim, modest house, the green car smoothly turned to the right, giving no clear view of the driver or the rear license plate. He'll be waiting, Nancy thought.

Midge eagerly pulled Nancy up the steps. "Pop," she shouted. "Look who brought me home. Nancy Drew!"

Nancy found the living room tidy but sparsely furnished. Mr. Watson was a thin, pleasant-looking man with a tired, lined face. He stood up smiling and extended his hand.

"I'm glad to meet you, Nancy. Won't you sit down?"

"Nancy may let me be her assistant, Pop," Midge said, grinning from ear to ear. Then she dashed for the kitchen. "I'll be right back."

Mr. Watson smiled. "You have to forgive her. You see, you're her heroine. She reads everything she can find about you."

"That's very flattering," Nancy said, blushing.

"Midge is a good child," Mr. Watson said. "A little too forward, but she has a good heart and she's bright. Since we lost her mother, she's been a big help to me."

Midge appeared with a tray of cookies and served them with great care.

"I lost my job some time ago," Mr. Watson said, "and it's been hard. I haven't been able to give Midge the things a young girl ought to have."

"Sure you have, Pop. We're doing fine," Midge put in.

As Nancy looked at the pair, she felt a surge of respect and admiration for them.

"You want to earn some money to help your dad, don't you, Midge?" the girl detective said.

"No, that wouldn't be right," Mr. Watson replied. "Whatever Midge earns goes into the bank for her college education."

As he talked, Nancy knew she was very close to taking on an assistant. But she needed more time to think about the responsibility involved.

"So," Mr. Watson went on, "if you could hire Midge, I'm sure you'd find her a loyal helper. I'd be very grateful and I'd trust you completely to take care of her. Your reputation and that of your father are the best in River Heights."

Nancy reached out and patted his arm. "That's one of the nicest things that anyone has ever said to me. Midge is a fine girl. But I need a day to think it over. I have to go to New Brighton tomorrow, so I'll call you in a day or two."

"Watch out for the guy in the mystery car," Midge whispered as she walked Nancy to the curb. Nancy gave her a hug and then drove off. Within a few blocks, the green Chevy reappeared and Nancy tensed behind her wheel.

I have to lose it, she thought as she moved along in the downtown traffic. But how? She was driving in the left lane and saw a large truck on her right, going rather slowly. She stayed next to the truck and waited until they came up to a bank building that had a driveway on one side leading to its parking lot in the back.

"Here's my chance," Nancy said to herself. She accelerated until she was ahead of the truck, then cut over to the right lane just before the driveway. A moment later she turned in to it.

"I hope when my shadow catches up, the truck will be blocking the driveway entrance," she murmured as she stopped the car behind the bank building. With bated breath, she waited for the green Chevy to appear. But several minutes passed and there was no sign of it. "I did it!" Nancy cried jubilantly. "I foiled him!" Quickly she drove out of the parking lot and sped home.

As Nancy pulled into her own garage, she pondered the mysterious sedan. Could it have something to do with Nina's case? Time would tell.

That night Nancy packed her suitcase while Hannah prepared a Thermos jug and more sandwiches and fruit than Nancy could possibly eat. Nancy protested that New Brighton was under a hundred miles away, and besides, she was meeting her friend Nina in a coffee shop!

28

"Well," Hannah said, laughing, "you never know, you might run out of gas, you might have car trouble, or worse—the coffee shop might be closed!"

Nancy shook her head, kissed Hannah goodnight, then stopped by her father's study to deliver a goodnight kiss.

The next morning she started out at nine after a last-minute phone call from Bess, who again begged her to hurry and finish the case.

As she traveled the lonely road to New Brighton, she glanced into her rear-view mirror from time to time. Ten miles out, the green Chevy appeared again! Faced with a long drive on an open highway, Nancy had little opportunity to lose her shadow.

Good thing I'm early, she thought. It'll give me a chance to get rid of him once I get into town. But if I do, it probably won't be for long. This guy seems to know every move I make!

When Nancy reached the outskirts of New Brighton, she drove around for a while to familiarize herself with the area. Then, in a quick, skillful maneuver, she escaped from her shadow through a narrow side street.

When she was sure that the green Chevy was no longer behind her, she parked in a lot behind Benton's coffee shop. Nina wasn't there yet, so she took a seat facing the door.

In a few minutes, her old friend appeared, looking tanned and fit. She wore her thick chestnut hair long now and her blue eyes were hidden behind a pair of sunglasses.

"Oh, Nancy," the young tennis player cried, embracing the young detective. "I was so afraid something would happen and you wouldn't come."

"Not a chance," Nancy said with a smile. "After all, what are friends for? Remember when we were little kids and we had our old cardboard clubhouse behind the Marvins' garage? Remember the secret handshake and the No Boys Allowed sign and how we misspelled it, A-l-o-u-d?"

Nina laughed, took her glasses off, and the two chattered on for several minutes before Nancy was jolted back to the present by the nervous, frightened look in her friend's eyes.

"Nina, you must tell me what happened to your dad and what threats you've been getting. I've been a wreck worrying."

Nina took a deep breath and gave a complete rundown of events. Her father and his partner, Aaron Calisher, had had a successful business dealing in securities. About a year before, her father had suddenly been accused of an illegal stock transaction that involved the fraudulent use of the mails. It was a complicated charge and Mr. Ford was innocent. But the proof of his innocence was in a small safe that had been stolen from his private office in the company building the night prior to his arrest.

Nancy tapped her fingers on the table. "That's a strange coincidence," she said. "It looks as if someone inside the company framed your dad and then got rid of the proof that would clear him."

Nina nodded. "That's what I think. Yet, the burglary was so odd that I keep hoping it *was* just a coincidence and that the safe can still be found."

Nancy pinched her eyes. "You do? What makes you say that?"

"Well," said Nina, "two men were seen taking the safe from the company office that night. It was a small box, weighing about three hundred pounds. The man who saw them was an off-duty policeman. He shouted to them to stop, but one of the burglars and the safe were already in the car. He apparently panicked and drove off without his accomplice, who escaped on foot. The off-duty policeman gave chase in his car and pursued the thief along the road to River Heights. Other police cars joined in the hunt but they lost sight of him for several minutes. Then they found the car abandoned in a small village on the first road that turned off the highway."

"And the safe?" Nancy asked.

Nina shrugged. "It was nowhere in sight."

"Maybe it was transferred to another car."

"Well, the fugitive did steal another car but a short time later he was found slumped over the wheel, unconscious. And the safe wasn't in that car, either!"

"That's incredible," Nancy said, "but since he was captured, he must have said something to the police."

"He couldn't. He died of a heart attack that same night."

"Oh boy, this *is* complicated," Nancy said. "And you say his accomplice escaped?"

"That's right, and he was never caught!"

Nancy was thoughtful. "Do you suppose the man who died transferred the safe to a third car somewhere along the way? But then, why would he do that? And if he did, why didn't he go along in that car? Why, as a matter of fact, did he abandon the first car?"

"Would you believe he ran out of gas?"

Nancy smiled. "Crooks can be stupid sometimes. Of course, he may have hidden the safe somewhere."

"The police thought of that, too," Nina said, "but they said he wouldn't have had time. Anyway, one man couldn't have hauled a safe that size."

Nancy swizzled her soda with the straw while Nina twisted her fingers nervously. "What do you think, Nancy?"

"Well, there's one other possibility. He could have pulled off the road for a minute and dumped the safe. But, of course, I'm sure the police checked the entire area."

Nina nodded. "There were twenty officers in the search party."

Nancy sighed. "Then it must have been an inside job. The people who stole the safe probably worked for your father. They staged the burglary so no one would suspect they were really only after the evidence that would prove your father's innocence. Maybe they even took the documents *before* they stole the safe!"

Nina looked shocked at first, then she brightened. "But my father was the only person who knew the combination, and he had checked the contents an hour or so before the burglary took place."

"So," Nancy continued, "there would have been no way for the thieves to have opened the safe before the man who drove off with it died. And since the burglary hadn't gone as planned, the thief who escaped on foot could not have known what happened to the safe."

I hope the safe is still somewhere along that road, she thought, and that the police missed it somehow.

"Well," the young detective said aloud, "finding the safe is my problem. But now, tell me about your dad."

Tears filled Nina's eyes and she swallowed hard.

4

Telephone Threats

Nancy tried to put Nina at ease as her distraught friend struggled to speak of her father.

"The police were taking him to the penitentiary in a squad car," she began. "When they drove across the bridge, the river had already started to crest over the top. A big tree trunk slammed into the bridge and the car was swept away in a flood of water. The police managed to get out of the car, but poor Dad, in handcuffs—he didn't have a chance."

"Nina, you mustn't think he didn't have a chance," Nancy said. "There *is* hope that he's alive somewhere, because when a body is lost in a river this far from the sea, it's found eventually. And since no one has found your father, I think the odds are good that he escaped."

For the first time, Nina smiled without tension. "Really, Nancy. You think so?" Then her face clouded. She was staring at something over Nancy's shoulder.

"Nina, what is it?" the girl detective asked.

"Please don't turn around," Nina muttered. "It's *them*. They mustn't see me."

As Nina spoke with fear, she hunched down in the booth. Nancy did the same, though she was aching to turn around to see who was causing her friend such anxiety.

"Who is it?" Nancy whispered again. "Are they the people who are threatening you?"

Nina shook her head. "No, they're the Calishers."

Nancy gaped in confusion. "The people you're living with? Why in the world are you afraid to have them see you?"

Nina did not answer right away. She watched the couple take a booth around the corner. "It's hard to explain, except that they've become nervous wrecks about my tennis game. Every so often, just before a match, they go to pieces worrying whether I'll win or lose. Then *I* get nervous."

Nina leaned toward Nancy and continued. "After I was threatened over the telephone yesterday, I wasn't too scared until Uncle Aaron—I call the Calishers Uncle Aaron and Aunt Emily—anyway, until Uncle Aaron heard about it. I thought he'd have a heart attack! This morning, I got another call while he was out and when he came home and heard about it, he turned beet-red. He started gasping for breath and had to lie down.

"So you see, I don't want to do anything to upset him. He's really been this way ever since Dad disappeared a few months ago. That's why I don't want him to know that you're reopening the case, much less that I told you about the threats."

Nancy was puzzled as she ran her fingers through her hair. "I don't understand the phone calls," she said. "Didn't you tell the police?"

"No," Nina said. "We haven't. No one wants to tell the police for fear it will hurt the image of tennis. You see, the man who called me said, 'If you want to stay alive, you'd better plan on losing your first big tennis match'!"

"Oh, my goodness," Nancy said.

"Similar things have been happening to other players since the tournament began last week."

Nancy knew that the annual New Brighton Invitational Tennis Tournament was already under way. The local club had long sponsored what had become one of the most prestigious and important competitions in the country. It was considered an honor to be invited to participate, and several of the world's topflight players came each year.

Nancy had always felt that the reason Nina and her father had moved to New Brighton was the fact that there she could get the best training in the country. In the past, Nancy and her friends had often attended the exciting matches, but this year Nancy's spare time was spent on plans for the River Heights Bicentennial and she had not kept up to date on the tournament.

"One player," Nina continued, "was delayed for a match by what turned out to be a fake phone call telling him his father was seriously ill. Another couldn't get to his first match because somebody put sugar in his gas tank and the car stalled. Both men were favored to win and both lost their matches by default. Now we think the same crooks are threatening me."

Nancy sighed. "It sounds as if some big-time gamblers might be involved in this. The authorities should be told what's going on."

"Yes," Nina said hesitantly, "I guess they should, but—"

"If the gamblers can throw a champion off

stride or prevent another from showing up, all they have to do is bet on his or her opponent and take the winnings. Have the tournament officials been informed?"

Nina bit her lip. "I don't know, Nancy. Probably not," she said, pausing. "I'll tell you what. I promise to do it as soon as I get home. I'll make sure that the officials know, if only you will help me find out what happened to my father and try to clear his name."

Nancy touched her hand. "Okay. First things first. I'm going to check in at the New Brighton Motor Lodge and start work tomorrow, bright and early."

The beaming smile on Nina's face brought one to Nancy's as she looked around the coffee shop. "Now, how are we going to get you out of here without the Calishers seeing you?"

"Well," Nina replied, "you could leave first. Then if I meet them they won't suspect anything. If we ran into them together, I'm sure they'd remember you from River Heights."

Nancy agreed with her friend's strategy and started to get up when the door of the coffee shop was flung open and Midge Watson came tearing in. She skidded to a stop in front of the girls' table.

"Nancy," she yelled, "come quick! Some

guy's been trying to fool with your brakes. Hurry!" Then she bolted out the door.

Nancy chased after Midge around the corner into the parking lot just in time to see the now familiar green Chevy vanishing from the opposite exit.

"I caught him trying to fix your brakes, Nancy. And I mean fix them so they wouldn't work! His back was turned so I couldn't get a good look at him, but the minute I shouted, I saw his right hand. It had an anchor tattooed on the back. How's that for a clue? Aren't you proud of me? Boy, am I starved. This looks like a great place to eat."

Still talking, Midge led Nancy back into the coffee shop to Nina's table. The Calishers, attracted by the uproar, had joined the girl. They looked confused, and Nina, obviously uncomfortable, tried to appear cheerful.

She reintroduced Nancy to the Calishers, who remembered her from prior years in River Heights. Nancy then introduced Midge and explained the reason for her unusual behavior.

Mr. Calisher, a thin man with watery blue eyes, sparse brown hair, and a nervous manner, stared at Nancy. He seemed curious about why she was meeting Nina after so many years. "It's a pleasure to see you again, Nancy," he said, and Mrs. Calisher, a plump, mousy-haired woman, chimed in.

"Nina has talked about you so much. We have no children and we've always thought of Nina as our own." The woman's eyes clouded. "And now she is . . . under such tragic circumstances. I still can't believe what has happened."

Aaron Calisher looked searchingly at Nancy. "I know of your detective skills and I'm sure you want to help Nina. But please don't try to reopen John Ford's case. It could only cause more pain."

"Mr. Calisher," Nancy replied, "I do respect your opinion. But Nina is a responsible adult now and she has asked me to help. As long as John Ford's disappearance remains a mystery and that safe is missing, we can't give up."

Nancy's listener reddened and his wife put her hand on his arm. He simply nodded. "I hope you won't regret your decision."

5

Nancy Gets an Assistant

Nancy was confident she had made the right decision, and Nina's eyes showed her gratitude and faith in Nancy. Silently, the young detective watched the Calishers depart with Nina after insisting they pay the girls' check.

When they were gone, Midge spoke again. "Hey, wasn't that Nina Ford, the tennis player? Boy, am I hungry. I could eat a bear. Can I order a bear, Nancy?" She laughed.

Nancy didn't focus on Midge right away. Her mind was filled with thoughts of the Calishers' strange reaction. Then she became aware of the girl's babbling and looked at her sternly.

"What are you doing in New Brighton? Why did you follow me to this coffee shop?"

Midge flashed a smile. "Didn't I tell you I was a good detective? I'll bet you can't guess how I found out."

Without answering, Nancy looked her straight in the eye and Midge knew the young detective was beginning to lose patience.

"Please don't be angry with me," the girl begged. "You practically said I was going to be your assistant!"

"All right," Nancy said in a firm and quiet tone that her father sometimes used with her. "Stop dodging the issue, Midge. How did you know where I'd be and how did you get here?"

Midge took a deep breath and cleared her throat. "Okay. Well, I got up early, you know, and I went over to your house and I hid on the floor of the back seat of your car."

"Midge! You did no such thing. It was in the garage! Besides, when I drove it to the front of the house, I put my suitcase in the back seat— and you weren't there."

"I wasn't?"

The pretended look of surprise on the girl's face almost forced Nancy to laugh. She wagged one forefinger at the tip of Midge's nose.

"No," said Nancy, "you weren't and you know it."

"Oh," Midge replied weakly, "well, I guess I wasn't but—"

"Now go on, tell the truth. I promise I won't be angry," she urged sympathetically.

There was a moment's pause while Midge debated her answer. "Okay ... I hid in your trunk."

"But the trunk was locked." Nancy stared at Midge in disbelief.

"Remember when you drove out of the garage and parked in the drive? You put your suitcase in the back of the car and started to get in. Then you put the key in the ignition just as someone called to tell you Bess was on the phone, and you went back inside."

Nancy nodded.

"Well, I was hiding behind the rose bushes right by the driveway. When you went into the house, I took the keys from the ignition and unlocked the trunk. Then I put the keys back and jumped in."

Midge smiled. "I know I shouldn't have done it, Nancy, but wasn't it smart? I mean, haven't you ever done anything like that?"

"But you could have suffocated."

"I was ready for that, too. I had a piece of rope that I looped around your bumper. Then I tied the ends of the rope to the lid, leaving it open about an inch. That way I got plenty of air."

Nancy leaned back in the booth and let out a sigh. She shook her head and looked at Midge.

"Was that really so bad?" the girl asked.

44

"I was careful, wasn't I? If I hadn't been there and scared that guy when he tried to fool with your brakes, you might have had an accident. Doesn't that count?"

Without speaking, Nancy stood up and motioned to her companion to follow her out of the restaurant. Midge looked back longingly at the menu but meekly obeyed. When they were out on the sidewalk, Nancy put her arm around Midge.

"All right," she said, "I'm not going to scold you anymore, and the reason I didn't order you any food is that there's a cooler full of scrumptious sandwiches in the car. In fact, I'm ready for some myself. That wasn't the most satisfying lunch I've ever had—and it seems like ages ago!" Midge's pout instantly became a hungry grin.

"I'm very grateful to you for your help," Nancy continued seriously. "But you must remember you're my responsibility. I can't allow you to put yourself in danger. I'd never forgive myself if anything happened to you."

Midge nodded and bit her lip. "I know. I'm sorry. I promise you I'll never do anything like that again." Then she grabbed Nancy's hand impulsively. "But now that we've got that settled, won't you please say I can be your Dr. Watson?"

Nancy rumpled Midge's hair and smiled at her. "Yes, you can be my Dr. Wats—"

"Yippee!" Midge exploded. "I'm a real assistant! Oh thank you, Nancy!"

"Now wait a minute," Nancy said. "Calm down. We have to figure out what you're going to wear while you're here."

"Oh, no problem," Midge cried. "I brought everything with me. My bag is in the trunk."

Nancy threw up her hands. "That was very resourceful of you! Well, let's check in at the motel and call your dad and my dad."

"You still call your dad to tell him where you are and what you're doing?"

Nancy nodded. "Yes. Why? Do you think I'm too old to be doing that?"

"Kind of."

"Let me tell you, Midge. No matter how old you are, your father will always worry about you, so it's only fair to check in from time to time."

Climbing into the blue car, the girls set off for the New Brighton Motor Lodge, where Nancy had been lucky to get a reservation. She and Midge were taken to a large and pleasant room. Typically for motels, it had two beds in it.

"Wow," said Midge, "I've never been in a motel before. They give you towels and everything." She turned on the television set. "Color

46

television! Can we stay awhile?"

Nancy was dialing Mr. Watson in River Heights. "That," she answered, "depends on what your dad says and how long this case lasts."

When Nancy reached Midge's father she explained to him how Midge came to be in New Brighton. Mr. Watson was relieved to know she was safe but was not too surprised, as Midge had left a note that said she'd gone to New Brighton to be with Nancy on an important case.

"I'd be grateful, Nancy, if you would look out for Midge the rest of the week. I have a chance to get work in another city where I'll be staying with friends."

"Oh, I'll keep an eye on her, that's for sure," Nancy said, glancing at Midge with a smile.

After giving the girl time to talk with her father, Nancy took down his out-of-town number and wished him luck.

"What a feast!" Midge purred as Nancy laid the contents of the picnic basket on a table.

After the early supper was devoured, Nancy talked at length about the three mysteries: the disappearance of John Ford, the missing safe with the documents that could prove Mr. Ford's innocence, and finally the threats to Nina and other tennis players.

Midge listened with great interest as Nancy outlined how they would proceed. To Nancy's amusement, her new assistant whipped out an old notebook and the stub of a pencil and began taking notes. Nancy paced back and forth as she related the details given her by Nina.

"It's not a whole lot of information to go with, Midge, but it's a start," she commented, then began to unpack her bag. "We ought to think about turning in early, Midge. This week's going to be long, hard work—walking, searching, and talking to people for hours."

"Won't bother me any," Midge said with confidence. "But could you call me Watson?"

Nancy laughed, then pretended to be very serious. "Harumph! Why, of course, Watson, old boy."

Midge clapped her hands. "That sounds great," she said. "Now what's the first thing on our schedule tomorrow, Holmes?"

"What would *you* do first?" Nancy inquired.

"Hmm," Midge said, looking up at the ceiling. "Go through the police records?"

"You're close, but we'll do that the next day. Tomorrow we're going to take a canoe ride."

Midge's eyes popped wide. "What for?"

"We're heading down the New Brighton River to investigate the place where Nina's father was last seen alive!"

6

River Adventure

It was still dark outside when Nancy felt Midge gently shaking her shoulder. "Nancy," the girl whispered. "It's getting light. Shouldn't we be leaving?"

Nancy groaned and turned over to glance at her watch. "Midge—"

"Watson."

"Watson, do you know it's only five o'clock?"

"Sure. Don't we want to get an early start?"

"Not *this* early."

"But it's supposed to rain this afternoon."

Nancy sat up. "I didn't hear any weather report. Were you watching TV all night?"

Midge looked sheepish. "Not all night. I had this dream and woke up, so I turned the TV on real low. That's how I found out about the rain."

Nancy and Midge took showers, then dressed and went to the coffee shop for an early breakfast. By 6:30 they were in the car with a full Thermos and a bag of sandwiches prepared by the cook.

It was a sunny morning, but Nancy noted clouds on the horizon and realized that they could build into great thunderheads by late afternoon. She and her eager sidekick drove out of New Brighton and were enjoying the peaceful countryside.

Suddenly Nancy sensed a car's engine roar growing louder. In her rear-view mirror she saw a dark blur become a green Chevy as it bore down on the two girls.

Spotting a crossroads ahead, Nancy steered her car toward the shoulder to allow the anxious pursuer to pass. But instead, the driver took a reckless turn across Nancy's left fender, and careened off to the right, nearly running Nancy and Midge off the road. The two startled girls were badly jolted and Midge bumped against the car window.

"Wow!" Midge whispered, rubbing the lump on her forehead. "My heart just tapped a new beat!"

"That Chevy seems to know our plans as well as we do!" Nancy said in between breaths. "You okay?"

"I think so—but someone sure doesn't want us snooping around."

"You still with me, Watson?"

Midge managed a pale grin. "More than ever!" she announced, and Nancy pulled slowly back onto the main road. Within minutes their car was at the bridge that spanned the New Brighton River. Although it was not very wide, it had a good flow of water.

"This is where it happened, Watson. The police car was headed in the same direction as we are. The river was high and beginning to lap over the roadway. The driver thought he could get across, but when he got halfway, there was a surge of water and a big tree trunk hit the bridge right about there." She pointed to a section of the structure that had since been repaired.

"The car plunged into the water," Nancy went on. "The policemen barely had time to get out, and claimed they couldn't find Mr. Ford in the darkness and confusion. It was a miracle they made it to shore. Mr. Ford was handcuffed and didn't have much of a chance. But we have to keep hoping he somehow survived."

As they sat in the car at the side of the road Midge stared down the river. "It's really spooky here."

"My dad says this river is deceptive," Nancy remarked. "The water seems very quiet along this stretch, but it's dark, with strong undercurrents. According to Dad, most of the people who live along here are a bit strange."

"What do you mean?" Midge asked.

"Well, the heavy foliage and rocky gullies make the riverbanks almost unapproachable from land. For that reason it was never developed, so the people who settle around here are usually loners."

"You mean crooks?" Midge questioned.

Nancy nodded, catching the excitement in the girl's face. "Dad did say outlaws have been known to hide here from time to time."

"Wow," Midge said, "this is going to be thrilling."

"Not too thrilling, I hope." Nancy smiled. "You can swim, can't you?"

"Like a fish."

"Still, we'll both have to wear life jackets to be on the safe side."

The girls drove slowly across the bridge and turned down a side road that bore a sign BOATS AND CANOES FOR RENT. After a few hundred yards, they came to a large, weathered shack. A loose wooden shutter provided shelter from the sun. A dozen rowboats and canoes were pulled up on the bank but no one was in sight.

Nancy and Midge walked from the car, Midge carrying their lunch.

"Hello," Nancy called, "anybody home?"

There was no answer, and Nancy peered into the darkened interior. A light wind began to blow and an eerie, creaking sound was heard.

Midge shivered. "Spooky, just like the river."

Nancy agreed. She circled the shack looking for the proprietor. A sign near the door gave the hourly rate for boat rentals, and the price for taking a canoe down the New Brighton River to another boat landing ten miles south. A small notice at the bottom explained that the strong rapids prevented a return trip.

"I'll just have to leave a note and a check," Nancy said. "The car's here, too, as security, so the owner shouldn't be too upset if we borrow one of his boats."

The girls chose a sleek silver canoe that looked to be in good condition. Nancy said, "We need paddles and life jackets, but I don't know about going into a place with the owner not around—"

"He probably keeps the equipment in the shack," Midge cut in. "And besides, we've paid for everything."

As the girls timidly stepped inside, Midge

wrinkled her nose. "Crummy. Not exactly a thriving business, is it?"

The first room held nothing but a battered old filing cabinet, two worn-out chairs, and a pile of clutter on the floor.

"The stuff must be in back," Midge concluded, leading the way to a second room.

The next moment there was a crash and sudden darkness. "Stand where you are, you thieves!" a harsh voice boomed.

Midge yipped and clutched Nancy.

"We're not thieves, whoever you are," Nancy said as calmly as she could.

"We'll see about that. Just come out here and don't try anything funny."

Nancy and Midge moved slowly out of the room to see a tall, heavy man replace the awning that had fallen. He turned to face them with small, glaring eyes.

"Then what are you doing snooping around here, if you're not thieves?"

"We came here to rent a canoe," Nancy answered politely. "We put a note and check under the rock in the doorway and had to come in here to look for paddles and life jackets."

The man growled and walked over to pick up the check. He glanced at it, then at Nancy. His eyes gleamed with a cunning light. "Nancy

Drew," he said, reading the signature. "Well, how do I know this check is good?"

"I'll give you cash if you prefer," Nancy offered, taking out her wallet. "Now will you please get us our paddles and life jackets?"

The beady eyes narrowed to black pinholes. "What do you want jackets for?"

"You know very well there are rapids," she replied. "Besides, it's against the law not to wear some kind of safety equipment in a boat."

Midge cut in, "And you don't have to be so tough, mister. You're talking to Nancy Drew, the most famous detective in the world."

Nancy motioned for Midge to be quiet, as the man got a pair of paddles and two life jackets from the back room. "Famous detective, huh? Well, I've never heard of you," he grumbled. "Just be sure you turn this canoe in at the dock downriver, and don't put any holes in the boat or I'll keep your car until you pay for it. And leave the keys."

Midge's mouth fell open and Nancy gave her the eye. "No, I don't think that's necessary. I paid you in advance and I left a deposit. I have no intention of stealing your canoe," Nancy replied firmly and put the keys in a pouch she had strapped around her waist.

"Oh, get out of here," the man snarled.

"You're giving me an earache."

After they had shoved off in the canoe, Midge, in the bow, asked, "Nancy, why was that man so horrible? What does he have against us?"

"Not us, Watson. *Me*. He *does* know me. But he thinks I don't know him. He's an extremely dangerous man and I'd like to know what he's up to in New Brighton."

"Who is he?" Midge asked, her eyes round as saucers.

"His name is Bull Tolliver, and I was once told he vowed he'd get even with me if it was the last thing he ever did!"

7

Capsized!

On hearing Nancy's chilling statement about Bull Tolliver, Midge turned around in her front seat so fast that she almost upset the canoe.

"What?" she cried. "He said he was going to get you? And he recognized you? And you recognized him? But you both pretended you didn't know the other? Oh, Nancy, I don't understand."

"Sit still for a moment and I'll explain," Nancy said. "A while ago I helped convict some members of a burglary ring. The police couldn't get any evidence on the man who received the gang's stolen goods—the fence—and they never made an arrest. He left town, however, because his business was ruined when we broke up the burglary ring. He was heard saying that he was out to get me. I never saw him face to face, and he probably doesn't realize I recognized him from seeing all those mug shots. Understand?"

"I see," Midge said. "But Nancy, what are you going to do—call the police?"

"When I get a chance I'll tell them he's here, if they don't already know. But unless he's committed a crime and we can prove it, he can't be arrested. That's the law."

Midge shivered. "It sure gives you a creepy feeling, doesn't it?"

"I'll say," Nancy agreed, "but we can't waste time worrying about what *might* happen. We'll just have to keep a constant eye out for big Bull Tolliver. Now, let's get paddling."

The girls stroked easily and Midge quickly mastered the art of canoeing.

Once on the New Brighton River under the bridge, they found themselves thrust into that dark and moody atmosphere they had noticed when they had first looked south from the road. The murky water was even blacker than it had looked from up above.

"A good place for sea monsters," muttered Midge, peering down.

The sun began to hide behind clouds. The

predicted rains appeared to be moving in early. After an hour of paddling with the current, Nancy felt the boat move more swiftly.

"The rapids," she called to Midge. "White water. Don't sit on the seat now. Kneel on the bottom and don't paddle unless I tell you to. The stern paddler steers and controls the canoe, but you need to help. I'll call out left or right and then you go that way until I say stop, okay?"

"Aye, aye, captain," Midge obeyed.

"If we can get upstream and go a little faster than the current, we'll have better control and not flip over," Nancy explained. "Here we go!"

At Nancy's words, the rapids appeared and the canoe went rushing ahead as the white-whipped water surged on all sides.

Midge squealed and shouted with delight and Nancy shouted back her encouragement. Almost as suddenly as they had appeared, the half mile of rapids dissolved into a placid stretch of water.

"Fantastic!" Midge yelled. "Let's do it again."

"Don't worry. There's more excitement coming up," Nancy warned. "Oh look, Midge, our first sign of civilization."

She pointed toward the right bank where the land sloped up less steeply. A run-down house clung to the hillside. In the front stood four curious children, ranging in age from about six to twelve.

"Let's paddle over and see if they know anything that might help us," said Nancy.

Midge stared at the children with an experienced eye. "Good luck, Nancy," she said. "They look pretty tough to me. I don't think they'll help us one bit."

"Oh?" said Nancy, amused by Midge's quick character analysis. "And what makes you so sure?"

"Trust me, Nancy. I've seen kids like that on the north side. They're trouble."

"Well," the older girl smiled, "I think we can handle four little ones without getting hurt. Where's that old Watson courage?"

Nancy steered the canoe in closer. "Hi children," she called. "How are you doing?"

The four urchins stood there, mouths slightly open, but did not answer.

"Mind if I ask a few questions?" Nancy went on. "I'm looking for a friend who got lost on this river. Maybe you saw him."

The children didn't move. They continued to stare. "That's the *look*," muttered Midge. "Nancy, these kids are up to no good."

They were now within twenty feet of the

61

bank and Nancy was about to paddle closer when the oldest of the group let out a howl. "Let 'em have it!"

"I told you," Midge shouted as all four children reached down and began throwing great lumps of dirt at the two girls. "Let's get out of here!"

Backwatering as hard as she could, Nancy managed to move the canoe to safety, but not before many large clumps of dirt had landed in the canoe.

When they were out of range, Nancy stopped paddling and looked back. The children were laughing and rolling on the ground.

"Why on earth did they do that?" Nancy asked.

"I don't know," said Midge. "They just think it's funny. We got a whole family like that who live near us. They don't know what to do with themselves so they throw rocks. I can tell the type a mile off."

"Well," Nancy said, "at least dirt is harmless. Anyway, my father told me about the people along this river. They have reasons for keeping away from the world and I guess their children grow up thinking that antisocial is the way to be. It's sad."

"Yes," Midge agreed, "it sure is. But it means

that if Mr. Ford wasn't drowned in this part of the river, he was in just as much trouble if he tried to swim ashore."

Nancy began to feel real doubts about finding any clues along this strange and moody river. But, refusing to give up, she looked ahead for other signs of life. Before the next house came into view, however, the girls arrived at the second rapids.

Midge found them twice as exciting as the first. She became so worked up that she shouted, "Ride 'em cowboy!" and jumped up out of her seat.

"Midge! Look out!"

Nancy's warning cry came too late. In her excitement, Midge had violated the most important rule of boating. The canoe overturned and both girls found themselves underwater. Nancy came up immediately. "Midge!" she called anxiously but saw nothing. "Watson!" she yelled.

"Present!" came a cheery reply. She was swimming on the opposite side of the canoe.

"Well," Nancy said, "let's tow it in to shore and get dried out."

"I'm sorry, Nancy." Midge apologized.

"I know," Nancy said, "but I hope now you'll believe me that it's not smart to stand up in a canoe."

"Never again," said Midge.

The two girls managed to get the boat into shallow water, then lifted it in the air and flipped it right side up.

"Boy, am I hungry," Midge declared. "Why don't we build a fire and dry out and have our lunch?"

"That's a wonderful idea," Nancy said. "You bring the lunch and I'll meet you up on shore."

"Okay," said Midge. "Let's see . . ." She stopped. "Ohhh," she groaned, "what have I done? The lunch is gone, right?"

"That's right," said Nancy. "The fish are having a banquet."

"Oh, I'm so clumsy," sighed Midge. "I could kick myself."

"Never mind," said Nancy. "Let's get a fire started." Taking her waterproof match case from her pouch, Nancy managed to start a small fire, which helped take away some of the chill. Clouds obscured the sun. Soon a brisk wind came up and the girls were beginning to shiver.

"How far have we got to go?" asked Midge.

"About two or three miles, I'd say," Nancy replied.

"It doesn't look like we're going to find anything, does it?" asked Midge.

"Well," Nancy said, "that's the way it always is just before a discovery."

Midge nodded and sat huddling close to the fire. Then she turned her back to it as she idly began scuffling her sneaker along the rocky soil at the water's edge Something shiny caught her eye and she dug her toe into the soil. Out came two metal rings connected by a chain. Fascinated, she leaned forward and picked them up.

"Nancy!" she gasped. "Look what I found!"

8

Outlanders

Midge's cry made Nancy whirl around. She saw her young friend holding up the metal object she had picked from the river's shore.

"Handcuffs!" Midge yelled. "I found a pair of handcuffs!"

Nancy took them from Midge's now trembling hands. She examined them very carefully and then read the inscription: "Property of State Police."

"Oh, Nancy, they must have been the cuffs Mr. Ford was wearing. He must have come ashore somewhere around here. He's alive!"

"Dr. Watson," said Nancy, "that is a brilliant deduction. We've just had the first big break in our case. I think he *did* survive that flood, somehow. And as you say, he probably came out of the water around here. But where did he go? And why hasn't he made any attempt to contact Nina? That would have been the first thing to do."

For a good half hour, they sat near the fire and pondered the questions. The sky continued to darken, and Midge pointed at the clouds.

"Don't you think we ought to get going, Nancy?"

Nancy looked up and nodded. "Yes, but where to? Where should we start looking?"

"There's nothing but woods," Midge said.

"Wait," Nancy said suddenly. "There is a rather well-worn path over there. See?" She pointed to a trail that led up from the riverbank and then twisted and lost itself in the deep pine forest which covered the hillside. "If he took that trail, or if somebody came down that trail and found him—well—then we'd better investigate it!"

Nancy placed the handcuffs in the small pouch around her waist while Midge covered the fire with dirt. Then the two girls began hiking up the trail. Rabbits, squirrels, and chipmunks made scampering noises, and a variety of birds chattered as the girls passed by. But there was no sign of humanity.

"Boy," Midge said, "except for this path, it

doesn't look as if anyone's ever been here before. This is the spookiest part of the trip so far."

A steep hill made the girls pant and they
stopped talking for a time. Finally they came to
the top and pushed through the overhanging
bushes. Suddenly an unearthly scream made
them jump in terror.

"Help! Outlanders! Outlanders!" someone
yelled, and then ran through the bushes. As the
screams continued, the girls heard other voices
join in until absolute pandemonium reigned.

Midge turned pale and clutched Nancy. "It
must be something horrible that scared these
people so. Maybe it—it's a mountain lion?"

"Take it easy, Watson. There isn't any
mountain lion."

"Then why were they screaming like that?
What scared them?"

"We did," the girl detective replied. "Didn't
you hear them cry 'Outlanders'? That means
foreigner or stranger. Folks here get panicky
when they run into somebody strange."

"And they think *we're* strange?" Midge
commented in disbelief.

"Let's find out what they're like," said Nancy.

Pushing further through the bushes, they soon
came to a clearing with several shack homes.
There was no one in sight. Only a few fright-

ened chickens clucked and fluttered about. A mangy white dog appeared from under a house, gave a faint "Woof," and then lay down in the dirt to scratch himself.

"Busy little place," said Midge. "Must be a lot of fun here on Saturday nights. Where is everybody?"

"Inside, probably," said Nancy. "Hiding."

"You think they're crooks?"

Nancy shrugged. "They're probably just simple people who can't get on in the outside world, so they live here in this secluded place."

"Remember what your dad said about outlaws sometimes hiding in this part of the world."

Nancy shrugged again. "They wouldn't think we're any danger to them. We don't look like police officers."

Without hesitation, she went up to the door of the nearest shack and knocked. There was no answer, but the walls and doors of the place were so thin that she could hear people breathing on the other side.

"Hello," Nancy called. "Please open up. We aren't going to hurt anyone. We're just looking for a friend who got lost and we need help in finding him."

There was no answer. Nancy knocked again.

"Please . . . please talk to us."

Midge pulled Nancy's sleeve. "Look," she said, pointing toward the corner of the house. A little girl, perhaps eight or nine years old, was standing there staring at them with big eyes.

"Oh," said Nancy. "Hi, honey. Can you help us?"

The little girl twisted her skirt with one hand and looked down shyly. Nancy walked over to her and gently took her hand. "Hello," she said, "I'm Nancy. And this is my friend . . . err, Dr. Watson. What's your name?"

"Sue Ellen, you come in here!" The harsh voice made the girls whirl around. A woman was standing in the doorway of the house, a crowd of children and a man visible in the gloom behind her. "You come in here!"

Nancy walked toward the woman. "I beg your pardon, we don't want to bother you but we're looking for a friend. A man, about six feet tall, with blond, wavy hair and blue eyes. A couple of months ago he was swept downriver in a flood and—"

"We don't know nothing about him," came the short reply. "We mind our own business. You should do the same."

Nancy felt a small hand touch her arm. It was Sue Ellen examining her watch with great interest. Nancy knelt down. "Do you like my watch?" The child nodded.

"Here, let me show you how it works. See this? This is the second hand. Every minute it goes around once. And listen, when I want to have the watch wake me up I set the alarm and it goes off—like this." The watch alarm sounded and the little girl jumped and then laughed delightedly.

"Sue Ellen, come in here!" the woman commanded. "And you two get going. And don't bother anyone else around here or you'll get in trouble."

"Yeah," the man added from inside the house, "you'll get in big trouble."

Nancy and Midge retreated. "That guy wasn't very brave," said Midge, "hiding behind his wife."

"Never mind," said Nancy, "let's go. "He might be one of the men who ran away from the law. Let's not stir things up any more. They're not going to cooperate."

The girls made their way down the winding path to the river while Nancy tried to figure out what their next move would be. They were standing by the canoe, ready to get in and shove off, when they heard branches snap behind them.

Both girls stiffened, fearing that the strange people had come after them. They turned slowly, then relaxed when they saw that it was only the little girl, Sue Ellen. For the first time, the child spoke.

"I couldn't tell you back there 'cause Ma would have got mad. But there was a man who almost drowned in the river a couple months ago."

"Did he come out here?"

"Yes ma'am. He came out right here. I found him lying on the rocks. I got Ma, and she and some of my aunts came down and they brought him to. They wanted Pa to bring him up in the house but he wouldn't do it. And none of the men wanted to help him because they was scared he was a cop."

"What happened?" asked Nancy. "Is he still alive? Do you know where he is?"

The girl shook her head. "I don't know what happened to him. Ma put a blanket over him and the next morning he was gone."

"Are there any other houses around here where he might have gone?" Nancy asked.

"Not around here. Sam Jackson lives down the river about two miles, but he's mean."

"Mean?"

"Well, not mean exactly. But he's mad because they sent him to jail once and he done nothing to deserve it. Not like my Uncle George. He robbed a bank once."

"Is that your Uncle George who was up there in the house?"

"Yes ma'am. That's him. They ain't caught him yet. You won't tell?"

Nancy looked at the child, who was so innocently revealing her family history. "No, Sue Ellen, and I thank you for helping us." Reaching in her pouch, she pulled out a dollar bill. "Here. That's for being so nice."

The girl looked startled. "I never had a dollar. I sure do thank you." Turning, she ran back up the path and out of sight.

Midge cleared her throat. "I say, Holmes, wasn't that a bribe?"

"No, it wasn't a bribe. I didn't promise her anything. She volunteered information. In that case I was just trying to say thank you."

"I know," laughed Midge.

"Okay," Nancy said, "let's hop in the canoe and paddle down to see mean old Sam Jackson."

The girls got into their boat and Nancy pushed it offshore. Suddenly Midge yelled, "It's sinking!"

73

9

White Water Rescue

The two girls stared helplessly as the canoe filled with water and lay with its bow down, hugging the bottom.

Then Nancy stepped into the water and ran her hand along the inside of the canoe until she found the hole. She shook her head, "It's a big one," she said, "about a foot long, I'd say. We just missed seeing it when we emptied out the water and beached the boat."

Midge bit her lip. "Boy, will that guy at the boat place be mad when he finds we put a hole in his canoe."

"Well, we'll empty it and pull it back to shore, and Mr. McNasty will have to send somebody up from the boat dock to repair it. We'll have to pay for it, I guess."

After getting the canoe on shore, they started out on foot. The girls were closer to the downstream dock than to where they had started out, but it was difficult to negotiate.

The banks steepened now, forcing them to walk in the shallow water. To make matters worse, rain began to fall, and Nancy became worried about not making it to the lower boat dock before nightfall.

With their main supplies on the bottom of the river, she didn't look forward to camping out in the rain. Her only hope was that they could reach Sam Jackson's place and that he wasn't as mean as Sue Ellen had said. Also, Nancy still had the faint hope that Jackson could tell her something about the fate of John Ford.

As the skies opened on them and distant lightning flashed, no place seemed to be safe for shelter. Nancy knew that hiding under a tree was inviting disaster, and sloshing through water with the danger from lightning was no better.

They continued walking downstream, hoping for an open area on shore, but suddenly the banks steepened into a sheer wall. At once the current quickened, the bottom dropped away, and they found themselves being swept along with the flow! Nancy's heart raced and she lunged to grab Midge's jacket.

"Keep together!" she yelled. "Hang on so we don't get separated!"

"Okay," Midge said. "Don't worry about me. I'm a water rat. But I'm sure glad you made that guy give us life jackets."

The current was strong, but the girls managed to keep themselves afloat and close to shore. Nancy's worst fear, as the rain fell and the thunder roared, was that there might be yet another stretch of rapids before they reached Sam Jackson's house.

No sooner had the thought entered her head than she could hear a deep rushing sound over the storm. Rapids? Midge looked anxiously at the girl detective. Quickly, Nancy scanned the banks ahead hoping for some escape before they reached the treacherous boulders that whipped the water into surging foam.

None of the rapids of the New Brighton were particularly dangerous for a canoe, but a person could easily be injured on the jagged rocks.

"Midge—if we can't get up the bank in time, float legs first to protect your head," Nancy shouted.

The noise of the water grew louder and louder and she felt the current grow even stronger. She tightened her grip on the back of Midge's life jacket. The girl turned her head and gave Nancy a courageous smile. "Don't

worry, Holmes," she called, "Watson is ready."

As the girls abandoned all hope of escape, they heard a shout in the distance ahead.

"Grab the rope!" came the cry. Nancy and Midge saw a tall man standing on the bank. As they watched, they saw his arm go back and then a long coil of rope snaked out over the water, a life preserver tied to the end.

The life ring splashed down ahead of them, and as they came abreast of it Nancy made a desperate lunge. Her fingers slid across the ring and gripped it tightly. Then Midge threw her arm through the hole and they hung on to their anchor, exhausted, bobbing in the water like fish on a line.

Nancy looked up and saw the man looming above them on the bank. The sky had grown so dark that she could barely make out his features.

"Hang on," he called. "You, the big one, you hold the life preserver and anchor it. And you, the little one, you climb up. Can you climb a rope?"

"Sure," shouted Midge. "Just watch me."

The bank was steep, but by scrabbling with her feet for toeholds, Midge managed to make it up the ten-foot bank to where the man could reach down and pull her to safety.

"All right," he called, "now you. Be careful!"

Nancy pulled herself out of the water and strained every foot to the top, where she flopped down on the ground next to Midge. Then she looked up at their rescuer, who was methodically coiling up the rope.

"Mr. Jackson?" asked Nancy.

The man turned to her. His eyes were piercing and Nancy felt a cold chill. If this was Sam Jackson, he certainly did look mean. And yet, he had just saved them both from the river's rapids.

"Come along," he said. Without another word, he strode away downstream. He was almost out of sight among the trees before the girls recovered and scrambled to their feet.

"Hey, wait," called Midge, but the man didn't slow his pace. By the time Nancy and Midge caught up he was in front of a sturdy-looking house.

He opened the door and motioned for them to enter. The young detectives hesitated. "Go on in," the man rasped, "you want to die of exposure? The temperature is already down to fifty-five. I've got a fire started. Go on."

"Are you Sam Jackson?" Nancy repeated hesitantly.

"What difference does it make who I am? If

you're fool enough to come down that river, you've got no right to ask questions, and you're lucky you don't feel the fish picking your bones."

"Well, sir," Nancy said, "you're right—we've been too frightened and breathless to thank you for saving our lives!"

The man said nothing as he nodded toward the fireplace. The wet and shivering girls sat down to dry out. Their host disappeared, then returned from another room with two blankets, which he silently tossed to his visitors.

"You *are* Mr. Jackson, aren't you?" Nancy persisted.

The tall man, who had picked up an armload of wood, put it down with a slam. He turned to Nancy, his face now showing a look of anger.

"Look, lady, I told you my name didn't matter. I just pulled you two half-drowned critters out of the water and I'm the one who'll ask the questions. Who are you and why were you going down the river? You're not just joyriding like most of them who come down here. Now what are you after?"

"We're looking for somebody," Nancy replied, "a man named John Ford, who was swept away further upriver in a flood a few months ago."

The man sat with his back to the fireplace wall and stared at them. "Well, you don't look like a cop or a bounty hunter, so what do you want with him?"

"I'm a detective," Nancy replied. The man stiffened at her announcement. "A private detective," she continued. "My name is Nancy Drew and this is my assistant—Watson. We're trying to find John Ford because he is the father of a friend of mine. He was being taken to—"

"Prison!" snapped the man. "I know all about him. They were taking him to prison. The cops got out of the car and he didn't!"

Nancy's heart leaped. "How did you know?" she asked.

"How did I know?" said the man. "I read the papers."

"Oh," said Nancy, "then that's all you know about him? We learned he came ashore just up the river, but the people there wouldn't help him and—"

"Don't know anything about that."

Nancy fell silent. Then she looked up. "Mr. Jackson, I don't care if you do get angry with me, but I know who you are. I believe that any man who keeps such a watch on the river and rescues people on a terrible day like today wouldn't let another man die. You *must* know something else about what happened to John Ford."

Nancy was taking a calculated risk, hoping that she would shock this strange man out of his reticence. She waited for him to speak.

"All right," he said, his voice harsh and threatening. "I'll tell you. But you'd better not be lying about being a friend or you'll regret you ever came down this river!" His eyes blazed and Midge found herself crowding close against Nancy.

10

A Friend in Need

The two girls sat with their eyes riveted on the man's face. Nancy cleared her throat. "We're not lying, Mr. Jackson. It's the truth."

"It had better be," he snapped. He threw another log on the fire and then began talking and pacing up and down the room.

"All right . . . I *am* Sam Jackson. Who told you?"

"A little girl up river. Sue Ellen."

Sam Jackson shook his head. "She's about the only human around here. The rest of them are like wild animals. She probably said I'm mean, right?"

Nancy nodded.

"Well, if I am, I've got good reason. I served four years in state prison for a robbery I didn't commit. When they found the guilty man they let me out and gave me twenty dollars and a new suit and said they were sorry. My wife died while I was in prison, maybe partly of shame. I came here to live because I wanted to have as little to do with people as I could."

Nancy and Midge remained silent, waiting for Sam Jackson to go on. When he simply paced and said nothing, Nancy spoke again.

"I'm sorry, Mr. Jackson. You have been through such an ordeal, yet you helped us. Now perhaps we can help John Ford."

Jackson suddenly slumped into a rough-hewn chair. He sighed. "All right, you say you're his friend. Here's what happened. The day he was swept away I was on the bank, keeping a sharp eye out. Lots of stuff comes down that river in flood time and I can often salvage things —like a boat or a piece of furniture. I furnished this house with stuff from the river." He waved his hand and Nancy saw a battered moosehead that hung on the wall, one eye missing.

"From the top of the bank I can see upstream to the point where you came ashore. I was watching you through my glasses all the way. Well, the day John Ford was dunked in the drink I saw him crawl out and collapse on that beach, more dead than alive. Sue Ellen came down and discovered him. And then some women showed up and covered him with a blanket, but I knew the men wouldn't let them do anything more because they're so scared they're afraid of their own shadows—somebody from the outside would totally terrify them. So that night I went up there, got him, and packed him back down here on my shoulders."

Nancy couldn't stand the suspense. "Then he's alive?" she asked.

"Just hold your horses. Like I said, I brought him here and I tried to fix him up. He was in rough shape. He'd swallowed a lot of water and had a couple of broken ribs and a broken wrist. I set the wrist in a splint and I wrapped his ribs just right. I learned that in prison. I worked in the hospital and watched the doctors closely."

Nancy nodded but both she and Midge were squirming as they waited for Sam Jackson to get to the point.

"So I fixed him up, but he had a fever and didn't really come around for about a week. Oh, I forgot one thing. As soon as the flood died down, the police came by here and asked a million questions trying to find out if he had survived. I had to hide him in a root cellar I dug."

"Why didn't you tell them he was here? The man needed medical attention and should have been taken to a hospital."

"A hospital," sneered Sam Jackson, his

mouth twisting into a grimace of disgust. "Don't you mean a *prison* hospital? I wouldn't send any man to a prison. Not after what I've seen. John Ford was better off here with me. Anyway, by that time he had no fever and his bones were starting to heal and he was getting better."

"So what happened to him?" Midge cried, unable to restrain herself. Jackson ignored her and went on at his own slow pace.

"It took about two months for him to get all healed up and healthy again. But there was just one thing that didn't heal."

"What was that?" Nancy asked anxiously.

"He had developed amnesia. The beating he took in that river affected his memory. He had no idea who he was or what had happened to him."

Sam Jackson paused. "I tried to help him. I'd read about him in the papers and I had them all stacked up here, so I let him read about himself. He realized he was the man whose picture was on the front page, but it did nothing to jog the rest of his memory."

Nancy shrugged. "Amnesia victims often withstand all attempts to bring back their memories. Sometimes it's because of a physical reason like a hit on the head, and sometimes it's a psychological one—because they don't want to face pain."

"Well," Sam said, "whichever it was in his case, I couldn't get through to him."

"I read that occasionally a familiar or pleasant face will trigger a series of remembrances," Nancy explained, "and the patient recovers."

"Oh please, Mr. Jackson," Midge broke in, "tell us what happened to him. Is he still hiding here?"

Sam Jackson shook his head. "I can't tell you that. This morning when I woke up, he was gone."

"Gone!" cried Midge and Nancy, simultaneously. "This morning?"

"Yep. I had given him a hundred bucks and some clothes and I told him he was free to stay or go. He left a note saying he wanted to try to clear himself of the crime, though he still couldn't remember anything except what he had read in the papers. He might contact his daughter. I just don't know."

Nancy sighed. "Did he take a canoe?"

"No. He must have walked. You can walk down the bank to the boat landing. From there he could have hitched a ride."

"How was he dressed? What did he look like when he left?"

"He was wearing gray pants, a white shirt, and my old red sweater. And he had on a pair of my shoes that were way too big for him."

"Anything else?" Nancy prompted. "Had he lost weight? Did he have a beard or mustache?"

"No, he was kind of thin when he got here but I fattened him up pretty good. Yes, he had a reddish-brown beard—that is, when I last saw him."

Nancy remembered Nina's father clean-shaven, with blond, wavy hair and twinkling blue eyes. She wondered what he looked like now.

"Mr. Jackson, can you help us get downriver to the boat dock?" the young detective asked.

Sam Jackson nodded. "But not tonight. The storm isn't going to stop and it will be dark in an hour. You try to walk along that bank and you'll get hurt for sure. You'll have to stay here till morning. I'll make you some dinner."

The girls looked at each other. Then Nancy, realizing they had no choice, said, "All right, Mr. Jackson, thank you. But we must get started at daybreak."

The girls were so exhausted that they fell asleep when their heads touched the pillows on the makeshift bed in front of the fire. Then Nancy heard Sam's voice calling, "All right, ladies. Time to get up."

Nancy and Midge staggered to their feet and splashed water on their faces from a basin.

At breakfast, Nancy gave Sam the pair of handcuffs they found at the river's edge. "You should have these," she said, "to remind you of your friendship with John Ford. They'll be safe with you in case we ever need them for evidence." Then the girls followed the man out the door and down the trail along the riverbank. The sun was just coming up and the clouds had passed through. The world was still very damp from the heavy rain.

It took over an hour of hard slogging on a rough, wet, and winding trail to cover the distance to the second boat dock. At last it appeared around a bend where the river emerged from rough country and spread out into a valley.

"This is as far as I go," Sam said. "You can make it from here, I reckon."

"What do you think we should do about our canoe?" asked Nancy. "We had to leave it on the bank with a hole in it."

Sam Jackson rubbed his chin. "Don't worry about it. I'll fix it and bring it downstream tomorrow morning."

Nancy smiled at him. "Sam Jackson, you're not mean at all." Then both girls thanked him for his kindness and shook his hand.

"You just happened to catch me on a good

day," he grunted. "Now remember not to tell anybody what I told you."

"Oh yeah?" came a nasty but familiar voice. "And just what did you tell this canoe thief, Sam? You might just wind up in jail again if you don't watch out!"

11

Good News

The sound of Bull Tolliver's voice made Nancy freeze. Slowly she turned to face the big man with the beady eyes, who had stepped out from behind some bushes. He had spotted the trio from the boat house and worked his way behind the trees to come up behind them. There was a sneer on his lips as he stared at the girls and their new friend.

Before Nancy could speak, Sam Jackson brushed past her in a flash and had grabbed Bull Tolliver by his shirt front.

"Don't you ever threaten me with prison, you miserable brute. Do you hear me?" He shook the huge Tolliver until the man's teeth chattered and the bully made no effort to resist. "And as for that canoe, I'll have it patched and down here by tomorrow—so you're not going to be calling these girls thieves. They couldn't help it if your beat-up canoes can't take the rapids."

"Okay, okay, Sam," Tolliver wheezed. "Don't get sore. Let me go."

Jackson pushed the whining boat dock operator back against the bushes and turned to Nancy and Midge. "If he tries to give you any trouble, you come to me," he said. Then, without another word, he walked back the way he had come and disappeared from sight.

"Does that sound fair to you, sir?" asked Nancy, almost sweetly.

"Yeah," the red-faced Tolliver grumbled, trying to regain his composure. "Okay, but I'm losing a rental on that canoe today, you know."

"Don't worry about that," said Nancy. "I'll pay you an extra day's rental and Mr. Jackson will repair your canoe, so that should even the score, Mr. . . . ah, I didn't get your name?"

"Never mind my name."

"Are you ashamed of it?" asked Nancy.

"No," the fat man flared. "My name's Willow. Paul Willow," he lied.

"Mr. Willow, hmm," said Nancy. "Well, I'll give you a check this time made out to Paul Willow."

"Don't do that," he snapped. "Make it out to New Brighton Boat Dock. That's good enough."

He glared at Nancy. "You really owe me for my time and trouble this morning, too. When my man phoned me and told me you hadn't shown up, I had to come all the way down here in my car to find out about my canoe. I figure you owe me ten dollars more."

"I don't think so," Nancy said. I just remembered that I left you a deposit. That is more than enough to cover everything. If you don't agree I can always call Mr. Jackson back to discuss it with you."

"Great," Midge said delightedly. "How would you like that, Mr. Willow?"

"Come on, Midge," Nancy said, taking her by the arm. "Let's call for a ride." She led her assistant away toward the boat house, where there was a pay telephone.

Bull Tolliver stood flushed and angry, not knowing what to do.

A taxi arrived a half hour after their call and took Nancy and Midge back to where they had left the car.

"What do you think?" Midge asked, as they drove back to the city. "Bull Tolliver must be suspicious of something—he didn't just trail us to Jackson's because of a canoe rental."

Nancy agreed. "I think he is, too, and he overheard enough to know there's a secret between Sam Jackson and us. The question is, *why* does he care? I can't help but think Tolliver might be tied in to our case with Ford somehow, but I can't figure where."

The girls returned to their hotel, dirty and exhausted, and enjoyed the luxury of hot baths and clean clothes. Then they collapsed on the beds and had dinner served in their room. It was the first time in Midge's life she had experienced such a treat.

Nancy watched her with weary pleasure as the youngster eagerly ate chicken, baked potato, vegetables, salad, and a double order of dessert and milk.

"I'm very proud of you, Watson. You handled yourself well yesterday and today. You never panicked and you kept your sense of humor."

"Thanks, Nancy," said Midge through a mouthful of blueberry pie. "And don't forget, I found the handcuffs."

"You sure did. Without them we might never have gone up the trail and met Sue Ellen and Sam Jackson and learned about John Ford.

"Oh," Midge said modestly, "you probably would have done that anyway, Nancy. You wouldn't have missed those clues."

"Maybe, but the best thing that happened was when Sam Jackson threw us that life preserver," commented Nancy wryly. "Now, we'd better call home. I've got your dad's phone number in Huntingdon, where he's checking out that job."

Midge obediently called her father, then Nancy checked in at her house and spoke with Hannah, since her father was attending a special meeting. "We're working as fast as we can so we can return home."

When they had finished, they rested while Midge watched TV and Nancy began formulating her plans for the next day. Finding John Ford was the number-one priority. Nina's suffering was heavy on Nancy's heart. But before she could continue the search, she wanted to go to the library and the police station to gather more details, particularly regarding the missing safe. If and when John Ford reappeared, he would be facing the bleak future of a prison term unless Nancy could find the key to clearing his name.

The next morning, as they were dressing for breakfast, Nina called. A new threat had arrived, this time in the form of a note slipped under the Calishers' front door. Nancy told her to bring the note and meet them for breakfast.

When Nina arrived, she was extremely nervous. "Honestly," she said, "the threats don't upset me as much as they do Uncle Aaron."

"What about the police?" Nancy asked, "and did you tell the tournament officials?"

"Yes, yes. They know. They say the police are working on it."

"Good. That should calm down Uncle Aaron."

"Not really," Nina said and took the threatening note from her bag. She handed it to Nancy, who studied it.

"Well," Nancy said, "this won't help us. Whoever wrote it used the old gimmick of cutting letters and words from magazines and newspapers so the message cannot be traced." She read aloud:

"Nina Ford, start losing. Lose your next match or risk losing everything. We are serious. One match won't hurt. Otherwise, what happened to your father will happen to you."

Nancy put the note down. For a moment, she wondered whether she should tell Nina that her father had escaped the river but had disappeared again. When she looked at Nina's sad little face, she decided to risk it.

"Nina," she said, "I have some good news. But you must promise not to tell anybody—not *anybody*. If you do, it might jeopardize my whole investigation."

Nina's eyes lit up and she grabbed Nancy's

hand. "Oh, I promise, Nancy! You've got to tell me!"

"Midge and I befriended a man who saw your father helpless at the river's edge. He saved him and brought him back to health. Unfortunately, your dad was suffering from amnesia and disappeared one morning from his hideout at the man's cabin. He could be most anywhere trying to put together the pieces of his life, and he's probably very scared. I hope it's only a matter of time before we find him."

Nina's face showed mixed feelings—joy that her father was reported alive, but sadness that he had disappeared again and was suffering.

"Amnesia," she cried. "He doesn't know who he is? What will happen to him?"

Nancy soothed her. "It's not that bad. He does know who he is, because the man who rescued him and cared for him *told* him who he was. But that's all he knows. He can't actually *remember* anything. He said he wanted to clear himself, but until he gets his memory back, he's not going to have an easy time of it."

The girls finally parted and Nancy again swore Nina to secrecy, reassuring her that things were beginning to look brighter. Then she and Midge headed for the library.

Nancy asked about the newspapers covering John Ford's accident and the librarian told her someone was reading those issues. She suggested Nancy and Midge sit at a nearby table and wait for the man to finish.

Nancy glanced in the direction she had indicated and then the girls sat down. After a time, Midge began to fidget, and whispered, "Boy, it's going to be fun at the old New Brighton Motor Lodge tonight. You know what's on TV? *Gone with the Wind.*"

The man reading the newspapers Nancy was waiting for glanced up and then stared at her. Slightly embarrassed that Midge had disturbed the man, Nancy shushed her. When she looked up again the man was still staring at her. But then he averted his eyes and Nancy could see that he was not reading but was staring into space, obviously thinking.

The man was dressed in khaki clothes and had a bushy black beard. His black hair was receding at the top, and his eyes were hidden behind slightly tinted glasses.

After a few minutes, the man got up, returned the papers to the librarian and was about to leave, when he stopped and stared at Nancy again. He looked as though he were about to speak when the sound of an approaching police siren made him freeze. Then he bolted from the library, leaving Nancy staring after him in amazement!

12

The Crashing Staircase

Nancy and Midge looked at each other. "That's odd," Midge whispered. "Have you ever seen him before?"

Nancy shook her head and stared for a moment. "Midge," she said suddenly, "you start reading those articles and I'll be right back. Something tells me I should follow that man!" She dashed out the library door and onto the sidewalk.

Looking frantically in all directions, Nancy finally caught sight of the bearded stranger some distance away. He had stepped from the curb and was motioning for a taxi.

Nancy's thoughts raced. Should I get my car? Then she realized that by the time she went to the parking lot she'd have little chance to find the cab. She started running toward the cab, darting around a parked car and waving her arm as she ran.

The taxi door slammed shut. Nancy's indecision had cost her precious time. Disgusted, she watched the car drive off into the heavy traffic.

Nancy returned to the library and explained her failure and disappointment to Midge. "What did you find in the papers?" she finally asked, a bit breathless.

Her assistant had scanned the articles on the accident and compared the details with what the girls had learned at Sam Jackson's. There seemed to be no new clue. "I'm sorry, Nancy."

Both girls had been unnerved by the black-bearded stranger. Had he been looking up the story of the burglary, too? Could he have been one of those involved, perhaps the accomplice who had escaped on foot? And was he now also trying to find some clue as to where the safe had been hidden?

Nancy returned the newspapers and thanked the librarian. "Come on, Midge," she urged, "we can't solve anything sitting in the library—let's get over to the New Brighton police headquarters."

The girls made some inquiries and were directed to the desk of a Lieutenant Nelson. He was a stout, red-faced man with a ready smile and was forever mopping his perspiring forehead with a red handkerchief.

"Good morning, Miss Drew," he said. "Lieutenant Nelson."

Nancy introduced Midge as "Miss Watson, my assistant," which caused Midge to nudge her and hiss, "*Doctor* Watson!"

"What can I do for you?" the officer asked.

Nancy explained that she was trying to find the safe containing the papers that John Ford claimed would clear his name. The detective got the file and spent almost an hour going through it with Nancy, confirming the facts she already knew and answering her questions. To Nancy's disappointment, he could offer nothing new.

"Thank you, Lieutenant Nelson," said Nancy. "Let me ask you one more thing. Do you think John Ford was guilty?"

The detective sighed. "John Ford was a fine man. The evidence indicated he was guilty. But my heart tells me he wasn't. If that safe is ever found, I believe his name will be cleared."

Nancy didn't push any further, as she did not want a discussion about whether John Ford was dead or alive. On the one hand, she had a duty to her client not to reveal that Mr. Ford was alive until she had had a fair chance to gather the evidence that might clear him. On the other hand, she would have to tell the truth about him if the officer asked a direct question. She prayed he wouldn't ask!

Nancy and Midge left the station a few minutes later and, after filling their gas tank, started off down the road the thieves had taken on that fateful night of the robbery. On the way, they quickly gobbled the sandwiches Nancy had brought from the coffee shop.

They drove quickly to the point where the police had last had visual contact with the getaway car, then Nancy slowed down and she and Midge watched both sides of the road for spots where a safe could be concealed. They searched every clump of trees and every high mound of earth.

It was slow and tedious, and it took them nearly the whole afternoon to cover the area to the point where the first car had been found abandoned. Then they retraced their route in the opposite direction, rechecking as they went.

Suddenly Midge called out for Nancy to stop. "Look," she said, "I didn't notice that before." She pointed off the road, where the ruins of an old church could faintly be seen through the trees.

Nancy pulled off to the shoulder and the two girls got out. Nancy saw an overgrown and rutted road disappearing into the bushes and trees toward the church. The girls pushed through the foliage and emerged in the clearing surrounding it.

They walked around the structure, which obviously had been destroyed by fire several years before and never rebuilt. The roof had burned through and the interior was gutted, but most of the floor remained. Cautiously they went through the charred doorway.

"Doesn't look as if anything has been disturbed," said Nancy. "No marks to indicate that anyone has been here, much less dragged a three-hundred-pound safe."

Midge nodded. "Sure looks deserted." She moved close to the edge where a part of the floor had caved into the basement. Nancy felt a tremor.

"Midge, get back!"

It was too late; as the girl tried to scramble back, the entire floor settled rather gently into the basement. It was almost in slow motion as the timbers gave way one by one with groans and snaps, but it was too quick for the girls to escape. After the dust had settled, they both found themselves sitting fifteen feet lower than when they had started!

When they had recovered from their fright, they looked around and saw that the walls were now sheer. No loose timbers hung down that would have enabled them to climb up. But

Nancy put on a brave face.

"We'll get out somehow," she said, trying to sound convincing. "First let's look for any evidence of the hidden safe." With most of the basement floor now covered by the caved-in timbers, their search was restricted to the small area that had remained clear.

They picked at the rubble without too much hope. A thin layer of moss seemed to indicate that no one had been in the basement for a long time.

But then Midge cried out. "Nancy! Look! Here it is!" She pointed under a large piece of sheet metal that she had just lifted.

Excitedly, the girls pulled back the metal and saw the safe, lying on its back, its door open and bent back. It was empty!

"Oh no," Midge moaned. "Someone beat us to it. The crook that got away must have found it."

Nancy was so disappointed she could scarcely speak. "It looks like it," she said slowly. If this was Mr. Ford's with the contents missing, all hope of saving him from prison would be gone.

Disgustedly, Midge picked up the door of the safe and slammed it shut. When she did, the dust blew away and both girls stared at the words painted on the door: PROPERTY OF ST.

Nancy laughed in surprise. "It's *not* our safe! This one belongs to the church. It must have been lying here for years, empty. I guess the authorities eventually returned to get the valuables and never bothered to remove the safe. What a relief!"

"I'll say," Midge agreed. "But we still have to find *our* safe, and we're stuck in a hole in the ground and it's getting dark and—"

She was interrupted by the sound of a car squealing to a stop on the nearby road. Then a car door slammed and they heard voices.

"Hey," said Midge. "Help's coming. Now we'll get out of here."

"Not so fast," said Nancy. "How do we know those people are friendly?"

Without another word, they found a door that opened into a part of the basement where the floor had not caved in. Quickly but quietly the girls walked through, closing the door behind them. Because of the gloom, Nancy had to risk shining her flashlight as they picked their way, looking for a stairway. Then, behind them, they heard cries of triumph.

"There it is! Down there! The safe!"

"Get a rope from the car. It's the only way to reach it!"

"Right, but where did those girls go?"

"Never mind them. They're probably hiding. We can handle them if they show their noses. We've got the safe and that's all that matters."

Midge nudged Nancy and whispered, "That's what they think!"

Nancy pointed to the far end of the cellar. Rickety stairs were still clinging to the wall, the first few steps missing. "They don't look as if they could hold a church mouse," she said, "but it's our only chance. When those thugs find out that it's the wrong safe, they're going to come looking for us!"

"Maybe they won't know it's the wrong safe. I opened the door again so they won't be able to see the name of the church at first."

"Oh, that's even worse," Nancy said. "They'll really be looking for us—they'll think it's Ford's safe and that we took its contents!"

"Yipes!" Midge whispered so loudly that Nancy had to shush her. They could hear the men clambering down into the basement and realized they had only minutes to escape.

Hastily, Nancy boosted Midge up to the dangling stairway. Midge hauled herself up carefully, keeping close to the wall as the stairway swayed dangerously. When she reached the top, she signaled Nancy, who pulled herself up to the first step. As she did, she felt the supporting bolts begin to pull out of the wall. With a prayer, she climbed as swiftly as she could. Just before her hand reached for the top she heard the angry bellow of their two pursuers.

"It's empty! They got the stuff!"

At that moment, Nancy felt the stairs give way! With a last, desperate lunge, she caught the post at the top and, with Midge's help, she climbed to safety as the stairway collapsed with a roar.

The loud noise immediately alerted the men on the other side of the basement wall.

"It's those girls, I bet," cried one. "Quick, through that door."

Nancy looked at Midge. "Run for the car," she cried.

"Shouldn't we cut their rope and trap them?" Midge asked frantically.

"We don't have anything to cut it with," Nancy replied, "and besides, they're already on their way up! Come on!"

Nancy and Midge rushed outside, knowing there were only seconds between them and their pursuers . For the first time, Midge looked scared. Panting, the girls reached their car and jumped in.

Nancy frantically turned the ignition switch. Nothing happened! She turned it again and pumped the accelerator. The car would not start!

13

A Familiar Voice

Quickly Nancy checked the gas gauge. Almost full. She turned on the lights and radio. They worked fine.

"It's not the battery," she said.

"Pull the hood release," Midge cried, then jumped out. "Trust me. And keep it in neutral."

She was still tinkering under the hood when the angry voices of the two crooks became audible.

Nancy was frantic. "Midge, I hope you know what you're doing!"

"Hit the gas!" Midge yelled. Nancy pressed her foot on the accelerator and the engine roared into life. Midge slammed down the hood and dove into her seat. In a cloud of dust, Nancy took off down the road toward New Brighton.

"Midge, you're a wonder," she said after they were out of their pursuers' sight. "What did you do?"

"Oh," Midge replied, "it was nothing, only a little mechanic's trick. When I saw that you had enough gas and it wasn't the battery, the next thing to do was to check the fuse box. But I didn't have time. So I took a chance and figured I'd jump around the fuse box by running a wire from the battery to the starter motor!" Midge smiled proudly.

"Watson, you're a genius," Nancy smiled.

"Well," Midge said, with unusual modesty, "not really. I was lucky." Then she glanced in the mirror. "Oh, oh. It looks like we're going to need a lot more luck. Here they come!" Behind them she could see the other car closing in fast.

"What now?" Midge asked worriedly.

Nancy furrowed her brow, then her eyes lit up. "Quick, Watson, look in the rear seat. Do you see that small bag? It's got some of my detective equipment in it. Empty it out, please."

Midge vaulted into the back seat and did as instructed.

"Okay," said Nancy, "now stuff the bag with anything you can find. I have an old sweater somewhere and maybe a plastic bag with some trash in it."

Without questioning, Midge did as asked and

109

then climbed back in front with the bag. The pursuing car was almost upon them. It attempted to pass but Nancy skillfully moved to the left and blocked it. Then it swerved back and tried to pass on the right, but again, Nancy prevented this.

By now darkness was falling fast. At last they reached a lighted area where a row of industrial buildings loomed up on the left. Nancy dangled the bag out the open window of the car and then, as they were passing under a street light, she threw it in between two buildings.

Behind them they heard the squeal of brakes. Nancy watched in the mirror as the pursuing car swerved to the left and made a violent U-turn.

"They fell for it," the girl detective laughed.

"Wow," said Midge. "I'm not the genius, Nancy. *You* are!"

"Elementary, my dear Watson," Nancy mimicked the great detective Holmes. "I had to take a chance they'd fall for the decoy and check it out. Right now they must be pretty furious."

The girls arrived in New Brighton with no further trouble. On the way to the motel, however, they stopped at a garage and had a new fuse put in the car. Later, after a hearty dinner and the usual phone calls home, they relaxed in their room.

Suddenly the phone rang. Nancy picked it up.

"Hello," said a man's voice that she did not recognize. "Nancy Drew?"

"Who is this?" Nancy asked, instantly on her guard.

There was a pause. "Nancy, this is John Ford."

For a moment, the girl's heart leaped, then she grew cautious again. "How do I know you're John Ford?"

"Can't you tell by my voice?"

"It sounds familiar," the blond sleuth admitted, "but I need more proof than that."

"All right," the man said. "Do you remember how I gave nicknames to all Nina's friends when you and she were little? I called you Happy because you were always smiling. And the day you got your finger caught in the water sprinkler I told you I'd buy you a milkshake if you didn't cry. And you didn't?"

Nancy laughed. "And you bought me the milkshake. Oh, Mr. Ford—it *is* you! But where are you, and how did you know where to find me?"

"I'll explain all that when I see you. Can you

111

meet me?"

"Yes. Where?"

Mr. Ford gave her the address of a hotel and Nancy told him they would leave immediately. She and Midge dashed out to the car. Within ten minutes, they pulled up in front of a run-down hotel.

"What do we do now?" Midge asked.

"We wait. I described the car. He said he'd meet us here."

In a moment, a figure detached itself from the shadows at the side of the building. A man came into the light, and Midge and Nancy gasped. He was the black-bearded stranger they had seen in the library! Could this be John Ford? Suddenly Nancy realized from his walk and from the smile that broke out on his face that indeed it was!

She opened the back door and Mr. Ford got in. Joyously they shook hands over the front seat and Nancy introduced Midge.

"I'm grateful to you, Midge," Mr. Ford said. "The only reason I was able to find you was because I remembered hearing you say something about the New Brighton Motor Lodge when you were in the library. And I'm grateful to you, Nancy, because when I saw your face, something clicked in my mind."

"You mean your amnesia disappeared?"

Mr. Ford looked startled. "How did you know I had amnesia?"

Nancy told him of how Nina had enlisted her to find him and the safe, and about their rescue by Sam Jackson. Then a thought occurred to her.

"Why did you call me first?" she asked. "Why didn't you get in touch with Nina?"

Mr. Ford frowned. "I was afraid to phone that number. The police might have tapped the line."

Nancy looked at him with sympathy in her eyes. "I understand," she said softly. "But Mr. Ford, you can't just wander around like this. Please let me contact my dad and you can meet him and turn yourself over to the authorities. I *know* he'll persuade them to reopen the case as soon as we find the evidence."

Mr. Ford shook his head. "I can't," he said. "I'm innocent and I'm not going to jail. If the evidence to prove I was framed has been destroyed there's no hope of clearing me, and I refuse to go to prison for a crime I didn't commit. Anyway, you and Sam Jackson are the only ones who know I'm alive, so I'm safe for now."

Despite Nancy's pleadings, Mr. Ford would not change his mind. Instead, he got out of the car. Nancy gave him some money and he told her he would be in touch with her or her father within the next few days. Then, before she could stop him, he vanished into the night.

"What's going to happen to him?" asked Midge.

Nancy shook her head. "I don't know. This is really a mess, Watson. If I tell the police, he'd be in danger. If I don't, he could still get hurt somehow. And what do we tell Nina?" She sighed. "Well, at least he has his wits about him. He managed to dye his hair and beard black since he left Sam Jackson's."

"We've just got to find that safe," Midge said. "And fast."

The girls returned to the motel and went to bed, tired and disappointed. The next morning they were up early. Nancy had an idea. She remembered that in their search of the road the day before, she had seen a place where the old highway branched off from the new one. The fork was barely visible and was blocked by a barricade.

"I didn't pay any attention to it then," Nancy said. "But now I think we should investigate the closed part of the road."

The girls drove to the office of the highway maintenance department. An elderly clerk shuffled up to the corner and peered at them over the top of his wire-rimmed glasses.

"Yep?" he said, making the word a question.

114

"Could you help us?" asked Nancy.

"Don't know yet," said the old man.

Nancy explained that she wanted to see the records on construction along the River Heights Road during the week the safe had been stolen. The old fellow shuffled off, riffled through some files, then disappeared into an inner office. Finally he returned to the files and then, shaking his head, shuffled back to the counter.

"Can't find 'em," he said. "Had a fire. They got burned up. A lot of things got burned up; others were misplaced." He stopped and waved his hands helplessly. "It's just a mess. Why don't you try the American Automobile Association? They keep better records than we do. And they don't have fires."

Nancy couldn't suppress a smile. She thanked the old man politely and got Midge outside just before the youngster broke up with laughter. "That poor old guy," Midge sputtered. "He's so nice, but so mixed up!"

The girls drove to the AAA headquarters but, again, they ran into a frustrating roadblock. The man who took care of the records was on vacation and would not be back until the next day.

"This is maddening," Midge declared as they climbed into the car again.

"What did I tell you about detective work?" said Nancy. "You need a lot of patience."

"Are you going to tell Nina about her father?" Midge asked.

"I don't know. If I do, she may tell the Calishers and then the secret would be out. If I don't, it may not be fair to Nina." Nancy frowned for a moment and thought hard. "I think I will tell her," she finally decided. "Come on, let's go over there."

When the girls arrived at the Calisher house, Mr. Calisher was gulping pills for high-blood pressure, Mrs. Calisher was wringing her hands, and Nina was in tears. When the girl saw Nancy, she rushed to embrace her. "Oh, thank goodness you're here!" she cried.

"What's going on?" Nancy asked with concern.

"We found a threat on the mirror," Nina said. Then she pointed to a short, lean man with stooped shoulders, who had just walked into the room. "This is Ivan Foster, a trusted employee of Uncle Aaron's. He came here to guard us."

"Tell me about the threat," Nancy urged.

"Someone wrote a message on the hall mirror with lipstick. It was there when we woke up this morning."

Nancy went into the hall. Nina frowned.

"It's not there anymore," she said. "Uncle

Aaron was so upset he couldn't stand it. So he scrubbed it clean and called Ivan."

"That's too bad," Nancy said. "What did the threat say?"

"That I'd better start losing matches. Just like before."

When the girls came back into the living room, Midge motioned to Nancy.

"What's the matter?" Nancy asked.

"I have to talk to you," Midge whispered. "Outside."

Nancy excused herself to Nina and followed her young assistant out the door. When they were far enough away from the house so no one could hear them, Midge almost exploded.

"Ivan Foster is the man who tried to fix your brakes!" she burst out. "He's the man in the green Chevy. I know because of the anchor tattoo on his right hand!"

14

An Exciting Match

"Are you sure?" gasped Nancy.

"Positive! And it's not just the tattoo. He has the same build, same funny shoulders, same height and everything. I know I didn't see his face, but I tell you, that's him."

Nancy leaned against the front fender of her car, quietly thinking.

"What are you going to do?" Midge asked.

"Confront him," Nancy decided. "We're going to tell Mr. Calisher."

Midge gulped. Nancy looked at her. "You're sure, now. If we have the wrong man, it will be very embarrassing."

Midge squared her shoulders. "Yes, sir," she said firmly. "I know that's the one."

"Okay, then, let's go." Nancy led Midge back into the house.

"Excuse me," she said to the guard, as they came into the living room. "I have something to ask you." Foster glanced uneasily at Mr. Calisher.

"Mr. Foster," Nancy went on, "why did you tinker with my car's brakes the first day I was in New Brighton?"

"What?" Mr. Calisher cried, jumping up from the couch.

"Midge saw Mr. Foster trying to disconnect my brakes. She identified him from the tattoo on his right hand."

Involuntarily, Ivan Foster hid his hand behind his body. "That's a lie," he snarled.

"Nancy," Mr. Calisher said, his voice trembling. "Ivan is one of my most trusted employees. This is impossible."

"No, it isn't," said Nancy. "Doesn't he drive a green Chevy sedan?"

Mr. Calisher hesitated and shot a look at Foster, whose face had turned into a thundercloud. "I tell you she's crazy," he snapped. "I don't have to take this."

"We'll see about that," Nancy said. "I'll call the police."

"Err, please don't," Mr. Calisher intervened.

"Ivan, you're dismissed from my service. You may pick up your final check tomorrow. I'm sorry, after all these years, but this is unforgivable!"

Foster, his face a mask of anger, started for the back door.

"Wait," Nancy cried. "First I'd like you to tell us why you did these things. Why were you following us, Mr. Foster?"

She moved to block his path, but the man was too fast and too strong for her to stop him. He brushed her aside. "You'll pay for this, Nancy Drew," he hissed. "You too, Calisher!" With that, he rushed out the back door.

Nancy went after him and saw him jump into his green Chevy, which had been parked behind the house. A moment later, he almost ran her over as he shot down the driveway. Nancy hurried to her own car, which she had left in the street, and started the engine. But by the time she pulled away from the curb, Foster had vanished around the next corner.

Nancy drove up to the intersection. There was no sign of the fugitive. She drove to the next corner, but realized it was in vain. Foster had taken advantage of the many small side streets and disappeared.

Discouraged, Nancy returned to the house,

where Mr. Calisher was beside himself. "I can't even trust people I've known for ten years," he wailed, as his wife hovered over him, fretting.

Nancy asked the couple if Foster had a criminal record.

"Not to my knowledge," Mr. Calisher assured her. "The whole thing is just unbelievable." He looked at Nina. "How I wish you wouldn't play today. These people mean business and you might be hurt. What does one tennis match matter? Look at you, you're trembling. And your Aunt Emily and I are nervous wrecks!"

"Ivan Foster may be connected with these threats," Nancy pointed out.

"Why would he want to harm Nina or us?" Mr. Calisher asked, growing irritated. "You say he's been following you and tried to damage your brakes? Well, perhaps he has something against *you*. You've made a lot of enemies, you know."

"There's no need to get upset, sir," said Nancy.

"Isn't there?" Mr. Calisher retorted. "You come to New Brighton and reopen John Ford's case when I warned you it would only mean trouble. You advise Nina to go against my wishes. You accuse one of my best men of a crime and force me to fire him. What else are you going to do to disrupt my home, young woman?"

Nancy flushed. She knew that Mr. Calisher was partially right. Her investigation had caused disruption, yet it was bearing fruit. But she could not reveal what she knew until she found the safe.

"I'm sorry you feel this way, Mr. Calisher," she said. "But I'm only trying to help Nina."

Mr. Calisher waved his hand helplessly. "Oh," he said, "don't pay attention to me. I'm sorry I got mad. But I promise you, if Nina plays today there will be trouble. I feel it."

"Uncle Aaron, I will not give in to those people!" Nina declared with determination. "Don't you see that's exactly what they want? I am going to play. But perhaps Nancy and Midge will come along as my bodyguards?" With a grin, she turned to the two young detectives.

"Of course, we'll be glad to," Nancy answered her. "We'll protect you from those people who are after you."

Midge grinned. "We'll play the enemy match," she added.

Mr. Calisher threw up his hands. "Well, if you insist, there's nothing I can do. I'm certainly in no shape to come along; neither is Emily."

"I understand," Nina said and kissed the Calishers good-bye.

Once they were in the car, Nancy looked at Nina and smiled. "I know it's been a rough day so far, but I have news that will wipe out all the bad things that happened."

"What?" Nina cried, her eyes sparkling with hope.

Nancy had decided that it would be cruel not to tell Nina about seeing her father.

"Oh, how wonderful," Nina sobbed. "But where on earth is he? Why didn't he call me?"

"Well, that's the bad part. He doesn't want to turn himself in to the police until we have the evidence to clear him. And he's afraid to call you because he thinks the Calishers' phone may be tapped. He's gone off again, but he promised to get in touch in the next day or two. In the meantime, you must not tell another soul!"

"I promise," Nina said solemnly.

When they arrived at the tennis courts, she went to the dressing room humming happily. Nancy and Midge accompanied her and, when it was time for her match, they took seats in the stands.

The young tennis player had won her first two matches of the tournament easily, but now her opponent was the dark-haired, smoothly muscled Rumanian, Marie Jonescu, who had for some years been one of the top contenders in her class. Lately, however, some of the younger players had been pressing her hard, and the spectators were up for this match.

The play began and Nina served a smooth, powerful drive that the Rumanian returned with a weak shot. Nina closed rapidly in on it and volleyed back to her opponent's left. Marie lunged and just barely managed to return the ball. Nina neatly put it out of Marie's reach with a backhand smash.

Midge beamed at Nancy. "She won that one, huh?" she asked.

"Yes," said Nancy, "that makes it fifteen – love."

Midge looked puzzled.

Nancy grinned. "I see I'll have to teach you tennis scoring," she said, and for the rest of the match patiently explained the rules.

To the girls' delight, Nina won the first two games handily. Then Marie Jonescu fought back to take the next three, and Midge found herself biting her nails.

But Nina, rushing the net like a demon, took the next four games in succession, running her opponent from side to side and finishing her off with overhand smashes that the Rumanian girl could not handle.

"First Set, Ford, six–three," the announcer said.

Nina trotted to the sidelines with a happy smile on her face; she looked up at Nancy and Midge and the two girls waved.

"Atta girl, Nina," Midge called cheerfully.

But Marie Jonescu came out for the second set with fire in her eyes. Nina failed to return the first serve. Then she hit an easy lob that Marie disposed of with an overhand smash into the corner. It sent Nina sprawling as she tried to reach it. She lay there for a moment, and then got up, limping.

The audience stirred and murmured and both Nancy and Midge stood up in alarm. But Nina resumed the match. Her game was off, however, and her opponent pressed the attack relentlessly, winning the set.

When Nina came to the sidelines, she was obviously tired and still limping. The trainer took off her right shoe, examined the ankle, and wrapped it. Nancy saw Nina wince, but the girl held both hands in the air, thumbs up, and Midge broke into applause, which the crowd picked up.

"She won't quit, Nancy," Midge cried. "She's

got real courage and determination."

Nancy rumpled Midge's hair affectionately as they waited for the action to resume. Nina won the first point and went on to take the game.

When she took the second game, Midge bounced up and down in her seat. But Marie Jonescu was not a quitter, either. She began the third game by again charging the net, and the stadium came alive as Nina accepted the challenge. The two girls ran back and forth, less than fifteen feet apart until at last Nina dumped a weak shot far to the left that the Rumanian could not reach.

They played on fiercely until Nina, by sheer force of will, won the set and the match. The audience roared, and Midge almost fell off the bleachers in her excitement.

Nancy was happy for her friend, but remembered Mr. Calisher's ominous warning: "There will be trouble — I feel it!" Something told Nancy that he was right.

15

Eavesdroppers

Nancy and Midge pushed through the crowd around Nina's dressing room and then rushed in to hug and congratulate her. "This will be something for Daddy to read about in the papers tomorrow," was the first thing Nina whispered into Nancy's ear.

As soon as the well-wishers and autograph seekers cleared away, Nancy and Midge took Nina home, accompanied by a policeman assigned to protect her if she won her match.

When the victorious player was safely inside, the two girls returned to their motel. As they crossed the lobby, they were stopped in their tracks by a threat from behind a pillar.

"Aha, Nanzy Drew! I 'av trap' you at last! There eez no escape!"

"Oh, Bess Marvin, cut out that terrible accent," Nancy laughed, instantly recognizing her friend's voice. "What on earth—?"

Giggling, Bess stepped into view. "I had to come. Hi, Midge! I assume this is your loyal assistant, Midge?"

"Yes," said Nancy, "this is Midge Watson. But what are *you* doing here?"

"I came to get you back to River Heights before the fourteenth because if I don't, that snobby Kimberly van Rensselaer will drive me out of my mind."

"What did she do now?"

"Would you believe she's bossing around everybody at the bicentennial office, even the chairman of the committee? And yesterday she wanted to call a meeting of all the ladies-in-waiting to be sure we know how to curtsy to the queen! Only she slipped and didn't say queen. She said 'curtsy to *me*.' I tell you, I can't stand it."

Nancy smiled and put her arm around Bess. "For now let's forget all about Kim, and Midge and I will take you to dinner."

"You can take me to dinner but I can't forget her. She haunts all my nightmares."

Nancy made arrangements with the manager to have a cot put in the room so that Bess could stay the night, and then they went to a recommended Chinese restaurant on the outskirts of town. When they were comfortably seated in a booth, Nancy told Bess what had happened so far, knowing that her friend could be trusted with the information.

Bess was happy about Nancy's progress but worried about the fact that Ivan Foster was still loose. "He'll try to get you, no doubt," she declared.

"I know," Nancy replied. "We'll have to be extra careful."

As they were driving back to the motel, the young detective felt a peculiar chill up her spine that warned her danger was near. She glanced in the mirror and saw the reason. A car was bearing down on them at very high speed!

"Stay calm, you two," she said. "I think we have an unfriendly visitor behind us." As she spoke, a gray car passed them on the left and then cut ahead. Nancy was ready, having slowed down in anticipation. She braked to a stop as the gray car came to a screeching halt in front of them and two men leaped out wearing stocking masks and gloves, black sweaters and slacks.

"Oh, Nancy, help," Bess squeaked.

"Take it easy," said Nancy.

The men didn't speak, but roughly pulled the girls out of their blue sports sedan.

On a hunch, Nancy said, "What happened to your green car, Mr. Foster?" The thinner of the two figures grunted nastily and his big, heavy-set companion snapped, "Shut up!"

Suddenly Nancy became aware that Midge was not with them. She tried to look around but was shoved into the back seat of their assailants' automobile, along with Bess. Somehow Midge had escaped! And the two crooks hadn't even noticed.

The thin man, who Nancy was certain was Ivan Foster, quickly blindfolded the girls and taped their wrists together, as the fat man drove back away from town.

To Nancy's surprise, the car had barely started when it slowed down and turned left. After a short time, it stopped. The girls were pushed out and guided along a dark, quiet gravel path to an old house. They were led up three wooden steps, through the front door, and into a sparsely furnished room. There each was tied to a chair and their blindfolds removed.

Then the two men took off their masks. Nancy saw that she was right. The thin man *was* Ivan Foster. To her surprise, the big one turned out to be Bull Tolliver, the crook who had given the girls such a bad time in his new occupation as boat rental manager!

"Okay," Bull leered. "Now you know who

we are. Maybe you remember me, eh? You re-
call the burglary ring . . . ?"

"Never mind, Mr. Tolliver," Nancy said. "I
recognized you the minute I saw you at the boat
dock. The police had shown me some very good
pictures of you."

Bull Tolliver turned red. "Very smart, Nancy
Drew. But you won't be laughing for long. We
know you found the safe and you got the stuff
out of it. And we want it!"

Nancy sighed. "You can't be serious. Obviously, if we had found the safe, we would not
be walking around with the money and documents that were in it! Don't you think that by
this time we would have gone to the police?"

"No! You'd want to look it over first to see if
you could use it to get John Ford off the hook.
You wouldn't go to the cops."

"You're wrong, gentlemen. But anyway, we
didn't find the right safe in that church. It was
the church safe."

"Don't try to kid us!"

"If you don't believe me, go out to the church
again. The name's on the safe."

The two thieves looked at each other. Then
Ivan Foster motioned to Bull Tolliver. "Come
on," he said, "let's go in the other room. I want
to have a drink and talk this over."

The men left. Nancy heard them go into the

next room and sit down against the wall. It was so thin that Nancy could tell they were not talking. Her guess was that they were listening, waiting for the girls to speak. She decided to play into their hands.

"Bess," she whispered.

"Yes?" Bess replied, startled.

"Listen," Nancy said, winking at her to signal her trick. "Listen, when the men come back, I'll make a fuss and say I have to go to the bathroom. They'll have to untie me, and I'll go in there. As soon as I close the door, you stage a screaming fit. Scream loud enough to make them both come to you. Then I'll get out and run."

Bess hadn't caught her friend's wink. "Nancy," she said, "that won't work. They won't fall for it. One will stay and guard you."

"I don't think so," Nancy insisted, winking so hard she thought her eye would pop out. "As soon as I get loose I'll grab their car and head for the police. We know the real safe is hidden in the basement of the old sporting goods factory at Elm and Main, so we'll have the whole case wrapped up and—"

"Okay, smart girl," came Bull Tolliver's booming voice from the other room. "Thanks for the tip."

The two came back in, with Bull looking

triumphant and Ivan looking suspicious. "I don't trust her," said the thin man. "I think she wanted us to hear her. It's probably a trap. I'll go and you stay here to guard them."

Nancy's heart skipped a beat. It was easy to fool Bull Tolliver, but Ivan Foster was more crafty. Fortunately for the girls, Bull *was* a bully and Ivan seemed afraid of him. "Nah," the big man said, "I say we both go. You know the combination to the safe and I don't trust you to come back."

"Then *you* go!" snapped Ivan.

"You expect me to lift a three-hundred-pound safe? Are you crazy?"

Bull turned to the girls. "You just sit tight. We'll be back. But if that safe isn't there, some real bad things are gonna happen to you. And don't bother screaming. Nobody's within five miles of here."

The two men departed, with Ivan still looking sullen. Nancy waited until she heard the car pull out, then she laughed. Bess joined in hesitantly, then stopped abruptly. "Nancy, what are we laughing about?"

"I sent them to the building right next to police headquarters!" the girl detective replied.

"That's funny, but what are we going to do

when they come back here? They won't be thrilled."

"We'll be gone," Nancy said, "because guess whose little face I saw at the window?"

"You mean—"

"Yes, Midge! I don't know how she did it, but she not only got out of the car without their seeing her, but she followed us here!"

"Hello!" Midge cried, as she suddenly bounded into the room. "Miss me?"

"Watson, as I've said before, you *are* brilliant," Nancy declared. "How did you do it this time?"

As Midge untied them, she explained that as soon as the men's car had started to pass them she had crouched on the floor. When the car stopped, she opened the door, closed it quietly, rolled down the bank, and hid in the high grass.

"When those guys took off with you, I was really scared," Midge said. "But then I saw the brake lights come on and the car turn off the road. So I just ran like a fool up the long path until I found the driveway to this old place — and here I am."

"Well done, Watson!" Bess exclaimed. "Now let's get out of here!"

The girls started down the gravel path. Suddenly Nancy stopped. "Wait," she said, "if we go out on the highway and try to flag somebody down at night, it could be dangerous. And if we try to walk back to our car, we might meet the crooks on their way back here."

"Then what will we do?" Bess asked, a little nervously.

"We'll wait for them."

"Wait for them?" cried Bess and Midge together.

"We'll hide in the woods," Nancy said and pointed. "Back there. When they find we escaped, they'll think we've gone to the police, and they'll get out of here as fast as they can."

"Are you sure?" Bess asked.

"Sure I'm sure. Come on."

Nancy led the two girls into bushes at least a hundred yards from the house. There they waited. A half hour went by and Midge and Bess were growing fidgety.

Bess giggled. "Suppose by some crazy coincidence they find the safe where you said it was?"

Midge and Nancy laughed. "If they do," Nancy said, "we're in big trouble!"

Suddenly, the girls heard the angry squeal of brakes and saw headlights approaching. "Here they come," Midge whispered. "Let's hope our plan works!"

16

The Villain Unmasked!

The big gray sedan skidded to a halt and, without turning off the lights, the two criminals leaped out and ran into the house.

"There they go," said Nancy. "Hold your ears."

Sudden shouts of rage could be heard from inside, then the men came running out again. But instead of jumping in the car as Nancy had predicted, they pulled out flashlights and began shining them into the bushes.

"You said they'd run away as fast as they could," Bess whispered, her teeth chattering slightly.

"Let's hope they've just panicked and will soon come to their senses and run," Nancy said in a low tone.

The words were scarcely out of her mouth when the girls heard Ivan Foster's voice. "What are we doing? They're probably in the police station by now. Let's get out of here."

"If I ever get my hands on that Nancy Drew I'll . . . I'll . . ." Bull Tolliver was so choked with fury he couldn't finish the sentence.

The two jumped back into their car, backed around and took off with gravel flying. Quickly, Nancy ran out to see which way they would turn. "Good," she said with relief, "they're going in the opposite direction from our car and don't think they'll return."

The three friends jogged down the road to Nancy's blue sports sedan. When they arrived, they found a police car next to it with its light flashing. It had stopped to investigate the abandoned car.

At once, Nancy told the officers what had happened. She furnished a description of the two men and the squad car drove away with its siren screaming.

Exhausted, the girls drove back to the motel and flopped into bed, too tired to do anything but make a quick call to Carson Drew. To Nancy's disappointment, he had not heard from John Ford.

The next morning Nancy rousted her friends early and after breakfast said good-bye to Bess, who was driving back to River Heights.

"I had a wonderful time," Bess grinned. "Just think, in a few hours with you I managed to be kidnapped—and escaped. Just imagine what could happen if I stayed a week!"

Nancy and Midge laughed, then Bess waved and drove away.

Nancy and Midge called the AAA but had no luck. The man on vacation had taken an extra day. He was driving in from Canada and might make it by late afternoon.

"Delays, delays," Midge fumed. "Now what do we do?"

"Let's check the Calishers. Something bothers me about what's been going on there," Nancy decided. When they arrived, Nina was still glowing from her victory over Marie Jonescu, but Mr. and Mrs. Calisher were their old, unhappy selves.

"Did you receive any more threats?" Nancy asked.

"Yes," Nina replied. "Last night the same man called and said that if I won again the day after tomorrow, when I play Patty Winston, I'd never play tennis again."

"Yet you're smiling," Nancy noted. "I guess you've learned not to take these threats seriously."

"That's right," Nina said. "I think he's bluf-

139

fing."

"He's not bluffing," Mr. Calisher cried. He was breathing hard. "These people mean business. You're looking for trouble, Nina. I promise you that these people are dangerous!"

He coughed and fumbled in his pockets. "Out of cigars," he mumbled. "Have to get some. Excuse me." With that, he put on his hat and went out the door.

After he had left and Mrs. Calisher gone upstairs, Nina asked if there were any new developments in the hunt for the safe. Nancy told her of what had happened the previous night and that she wanted to check out the old highway.

"Have you heard any more from Daddy?" the young tennis star asked, biting her lip.

"No," replied Nancy gently, "but don't worry. He'll call us. I know."

"Can't I talk to him?" Nina's eyes were pleading.

"I'll try to arrange it with him when he contacts me."

Suddenly the phone rang and Nancy looked at Nina. "Is there an extension?" she inquired.

"In the kitchen," Nina said.

As Nina picked up the living room phone, Nancy ran into the kitchen. Softly she lifted the receiver and listened.

"This is your last warning, Nina Ford," came

a rasping voice. "You have to lose this next match. There's too much money riding on it. You win and I promise you, you'll never walk again. I promise you that."

There was a click and the caller was gone. Nancy rushed in to Nina. "Isn't there something familiar about that voice?" she asked.

Nina shook her head. "I don't think so," she said.

"Well, it's obviously distorted. There's something about the way the man speaks...." Nancy shook her head. "I can't place it."

"Say," Nina suddenly said, "where's Midge?"

Nancy looked around. "I don't know. She wasn't in the kitchen. Midge—Midge?" she called out, but there was no answer.

"Maybe she also went to the store," Nancy said. "She was running out of bubblegum."

At that moment, Mr. Calisher returned with his cigars. When asked if he had seen Midge, he shook his head and went upstairs to his study.

A few moments later, Midge came through the front door, whistling. "Hi," she said, "just picked up some bubblegum and chocolate."

Nancy laughed, "Well, I'm glad. I thought you had vanished into thin air."

At that moment, Nina excused herself to make a phone call. Once she had left, Midge turned

141

her bright eyes on Nancy. "Holmes," she said softly, "while I was out, did anyone call?"

"Yes," Nancy said. "How did you know?"

"Nancy, I know who's threatening Nina. It's Mr. Calisher!"

Nancy sat staring at her. "That's why the voice sounded familiar to me! Oh, this is awful. Poor Nina—betrayed by the very people who supposedly have been caring for her!"

"I followed him," Midge explained. "Not because I suspected him. I was just practicing trailing somebody. But then I saw him go into a phone booth and take out his handkerchief and put it over the mouthpiece."

"To distort his voice," Nancy murmured.

"I sneaked up close, behind a tree, and I could hear him, Nancy," Midge went on. "I heard everything."

"Good work, Watson. But I wish it hadn't been Mr. Calisher. Why in the world did he do it?" Nancy's brain was working on the possibilities. The firm of Ford and Calisher had been prosperous. It didn't seem possible that Mr. Calisher needed to win money by illegal gambling and fixing tennis matches. Yet that's what he was doing.

"What are you going to tell Nina?" Midge asked.

"I don't know. We have no real hard evidence

against Aaron Calisher that would hold up in court. To unmask him now could ruin everything. Yet, how can I allow Nina to stay in this house?"

At that moment, Nina came back into the living room.

"You two look glum," she noted. "What's the matter, has something happened?"

Nancy stood up. "Yes, something *has* happened, Nina, and I have to talk with you about it. It's a break in the case."

"About the safe?" said Nina, excitedly. "Or about Dad?"

"Neither," Nancy replied. "It's about the people threatening you. Let's take a ride and I'll tell you."

"Well, shouldn't we tell Uncle Aaron, too? It would relieve his mind."

Nancy hesitated and looked at Midge. "He already knows," Midge murmured.

"What?" Nina looked confused and Nancy put an arm around her friend's shoulders. "He doesn't exactly *know*, Nina, but it's too complicated to explain here. Please, let's take a ride."

Puzzled, the girl followed Nancy and Midge to their car. They drove to a nearby park and pulled up close to a lake on which swans were floating. Then Nancy turned to Nina.

"What I have to tell you will come as a shock

to you. That's why we had to talk in private. You see, we have found the man who's been threatening you. It's somebody you know."

Nina turned white and her lips trembled. "What do you mean, Nancy?"

"Aaron Calisher is the person threatening you," Nancy went on. "Midge trailed him to a phone booth a little while ago. She heard him. She also saw him put a handkerchief over the mouthpiece to distort his voice."

Nina was stunned. Then a tear forced its way from her tightly closed eyes. "I can't believe it!" she cried. "I can't believe it! Uncle Aaron. But why?"

Nancy put her arm around her friend. "That's what we don't know yet. Perhaps he's in debt. Perhaps the company is failing. The answer, I suspect, is that he needs money, so he bet on the tennis games and is trying to fix them."

Nina took the tissue that Nancy handed her and wiped her tears. Then she took a deep breath. "Well," she said, trying to get control over her voice, "what are we going to do?"

Nancy sighed. "I don't know," she answered. "If you stay in his house, you could be in great danger. But if we move you out now, he'll know we suspect him. And we can't report him to the police until we have evidence. Right now it's just our word against his. It would be difficult to prove anything in court."

"I'll stay," Nina decided.

The girl detective looked at her friend and saw a determined look in Nina's eyes.

"You're sure?" Nancy asked.

"Yes," Nina replied. "I'm sure. I'll stay and I'll try to do a good acting job until you can get the evidence you need. This makes me wonder whether Uncle—I mean Mr. Calisher didn't have something to do with framing my father. If he's capable of doing this to me, what else may he have done?"

Nancy agreed. "That's a very strong possibility. He could have framed your father and he could have arranged to have had that safe stolen. Ivan Foster could have been working under his orders all along."

"All that business of not wanting to go to the police and firing Foster instead would fit right in," Midge said excitedly. "He may have pretended to have those spells, and threatened a nervous breakdown to cover up his tracks."

"Perhaps," said Nancy, "but then he *is* a very nervous, emotional man. My dad already warned us. So maybe it was half faked and half real. Anyway, we have to find out. Nina, if you're brave enough to go back and stay there, we'll have a much better chance to get to the bottom of this mystery."

"I'll do it," said Nina. "I don't think he would have the nerve to do anything violent."

"Neither do I," said Nancy, "but just in case, I'm going to tell the police of our suspicions so they can keep watch on you and on the house the next few days."

With that settled, Nancy drove Nina home, then immediately went to police headquarters, where she outlined the facts to Lieutenant Nelson. He listened in astonishment.

"Well, Nancy," he said, "this is certainly serious. I agree with you that there is cause to keep a watch on Nina and be sure no harm comes to her. But your evidence against Mr. Calisher is very thin. We can't arrest him on that. Besides, as you say, if we tip him off, even watching him openly, it might ruin any chance of finding out what's behind these threats. However, we will follow him discreetly."

Lieutenant Nelson looked at the girl detective searchingly. "By the way, any progress in your hunt for the safe?"

Nancy told him that so far she had had no more luck than the police but that she was not giving up. Then she thanked him, said goodbye, and made a phone call to the AAA, finding out their man had finally returned from his vacation.

"Yes," the AAA man told Nancy when they arrived at his office. "There was construction on that highway on the date you gave me, until nearly midnight." He indicated the position on his map. "The main road was blocked and traffic was detoured down the old road here for a distance of about a mile. Then the barricades were switched and the old road was sealed off."

Nancy was encouraged. "Thank you very, very much," she said. Then she turned to Midge. "Come on, Watson. We've got another chance!"

17

Discouraged Detectives

As Nancy ran for the car, Midge tagged along like a tail on a kite. "Wait, Nancy—what are you so excited about?" she cried. "Do you think . . . ?" Then she suddenly stopped. "Oh, I see!"

Midge jumped in the car as Nancy started the engine. "I know," she said. "You think the crook went down the detour that night and dumped the safe somewhere along the road. Then the next day, when a different shift of police made the search, the detour was closed off and that's why they didn't find anything?"

"You guessed it!" Nancy said. "Oh, Midge, keep your fingers crossed that we're right. Because if we are, we can wrap up this case in a day."

As the girls drove out of town, Nancy looked in the mirror. The gray sedan was behind them again!

"We're being followed," she warned.

"Aw, just outrun them, Nancy."

"I can't, Watson. To exceed the speed limit is both illegal and dangerous. We'll have to think of something else."

Midge nodded.

A few minutes later, Nancy turned right and drove at moderate speed until she saw a parking garage she had noticed earlier. She knew it had two entrances. Smoothly she turned into the garage, drove through the gate, and handed the attendant money for a half hour.

"I'm going right out the other side," she said. The startled attendant stared after her as she zoomed up the other ramp and disappeared onto the opposite street.

To be certain she had shaken her shadow, Nancy made a quick left and then a right, then pulled into a carwash. A few minutes later she emerged on another street.

"That should do it." She laughed. "And we even had the car cleaned! Now let's find that safe!"

Nancy sped out along the River Heights Road, keeping a careful eye on the mirror even though she was convinced that she had thrown off their pursuer.

In about a half hour, they reached the point where the detour was. The girls surveyed the barricade of timber and rocks that had been erected, and groaned. It would be impossible to move!

They drove up to it and stopped. Then they got out of the car.

"We'll have to leave it here and walk," Midge declared.

"Yes, we could do that," said Nancy. "But if our shadow gets the idea that we came here for another look, he'll spot the car and we'll be in real trouble. Somehow, we've got to find a way around this roadblock!"

The girls carefully explored the ground around the barricade. It was covered with small, sharp rocks as well as fairly large ones. Nancy decided to risk driving over them. The girls got back in the car and she moved carefully to the right, through high weeds and over rugged ground. She heard the rocks scrape along the bottom of the car and prayed that they would not rip a hole in the oil pan.

However, the blue sports sedan reached level ground on the old road without any noticeable sign of damage. The girls jumped out and fluffed up the high weeds so that no one could tell that a car had recently driven through.

When they were finished, Nancy shook her head. "Not too good a job. If Ivan comes along and stops, he's going to see the tire marks." She thought a moment. "Well, it can't be helped. We don't have the time to do a complete landscaping job. Let's go."

The girls drove slowly along the deserted road, scanning the sides. They stopped at each small hump in the ground, got out, and poked it with sticks to be sure it was not a covering for the missing safe.

"Watch for places where the ground seems sunken, too," Nancy said. "Because whenever something heavy is buried, it settles, and after a while it's easy to spot."

Midge nodded and kept her eyes glued to the road. "There's a building," she called, pointing to a weathered one-room schoolhouse that had once been painted white. Its windows and doors were gone and in the yard stood a flagpole, rotted and worn and leaning at a crazy angle.

"Let's look in there," Nancy decided. She parked and the girls made their way up the old cinder path, through the weeds and bushes. They looked for signs of automobile tire tracks but could find none.

"I don't think anyone has been here for many

years," Nancy said. "But we'll peek inside anyway, just to be sure."

Cautiously, they entered the building. "Remember the old church," Nancy warned. "There probably isn't a basement in this school, but I don't want us falling through the floor again."

The floor proved solid, however, and when the young detectives were inside they found nothing more than a nostalgic scene from the past—rows of old desks and rubbish scattered on the floor, including a forgotten pair of small galoshes.

"Look, Nancy," Midge said, "some kid had the last word." She pointed at the blackboard where a faint message could still be read: "Miss Marshall is a mean teacher!"

Next to the words was an uncomplimentary drawing of Miss Marshall. Nancy smiled and was about to comment, when she was stopped by a heavy crash from outside.

"It's them!" Midge whispered. The girls ducked low and inched over to a window.

Nancy cautiously peeked outside. "Oh no." She groaned.

"Well *is* it?" Midge asked, her eyes wide.

"No," Nancy replied. "It's no one. But my car will never be the same. Look."

Midge looked. The ancient flagpole, which had been leaning so dangerously, had at last toppled over, landing on the hood of the shiny blue sedan.

The girls ran out to inspect the damage. They lifted the pole from the car and dragged it to one side. Then Midge inspected the dent with a professional eye.

"Well, I'd say that Morton could fix this up for about fifty bucks in his body shop. There's a big dent but no real damage. Just hammer it straight and touch up the paint."

"Thank you, Watson." Nancy had to grin at Midge's quick and efficient appraisal. Then she looked anxiously at the sky. The sun was getting close to the horizon. "We don't have much time. Let's go on," she said.

Resuming the search, the girls drove over a small stream. Nancy stopped on the culvert that passed under the road. There was a tiny pond on the right with crystal clear water. "Any sign of the safe in there?" she asked Midge.

"Nope," said Midge. "I can see the bottom and all around. There's nothing there."

Nancy looked out to the left, where the water flowed out in a tiny trickle. The ditch was empty. Sighing, she drove on.

Within a half mile, Nancy suddenly braked to

a stop. "Watson, down there!" She pointed to a steep incline. "Doesn't that look like a break in the rocks? Maybe a cave?"

"It sure does," said Midge, jumping out of the car. Nancy followed. They made their way down the slope, holding on to the bushes to brake their descent. If the thief had been able to stop here, it would have been relatively easy for him to tumble the safe down the little hill and straight into the cave entrance. Excited, the girls slid and slipped the last few feet. Nancy took out her flashlight and led the way.

The cave was barely five feet high but more than twice as wide. But as the girls moved cautiously into it, the ground suddenly dipped, and they slid down a wet clay surface without handholds.

"Nancy!" Midge screamed.

Desperately the older girl threw one arm around her protégée and then, somehow, managed to grab an outcropping of rock. Luckily her flashlight was hooked to the belt of her jeans. Otherwise they would have been plunged into complete darkness.

As Midge finally managed to find a handhold, Nancy reached down and shone the light into the direction of their descent. To her relief, the steep slope ended less than five feet below

them. Carefully, she and Midge lowered themselves the rest of the way.

Nancy shone her light around the cave. There was no sign of the safe.

"Nancy," Midge said, "there's not much that really scares me . . . but sliding down a black hole into nowhere—*that* scares me. Let's get out of here! It's only another wild goose chase anyway."

"I'm afraid so," the girl detective admitted. "But going back may not be easy." She shone the light up the steep, slippery clay slope. Along the walls jagged rocks stuck out, offering support.

"Look around for a couple of small, sharp stones, Watson. We can use them to dig small grooves in the clay."

Midge did as asked and in a few minutes Nancy was inching her way up, chipping out toeholds with one hand while feeling for the jagged rocks with the other. Midge followed in her tracks. Finally they arrived on top, breathing hard and smeared with red clay.

"I don't think we'll *ever* find that safe," Midge said, discouraged.

Nancy put her arm around the girl as they got into their car. "Never say never, Watson. We're not quitters. We'll find it."

"How?"

"I don't know yet. But we will."

The girls continued to the end of the old road without finding another nook or cranny to explore. To their relief, the barricade here proved less difficult to navigate than the first one.

"We should have come in on this end, instead of almost wrecking the car on the other roadblock," Nancy said.

Midge grinned impishly. "I'm glad you're not perfect all the time. I wouldn't be able to stand it!"

18

An Important Clue

Back at the motel, the two girls spent almost an hour bathing and scrubbing off the dirt and grime they had accumulated in their adventure in the cave. They ate dinner listlessly, not finding very much to talk about, but their minds were working, trying to figure out the next step.

Finally Nancy forced a smile. "Watson, I know you must feel bad, since you're not eating much. But cheer up. We just need to recharge our batteries and we'll get some new and brilliant ideas, you'll see."

"We will?" Midge asked and grinned.

"Yes, we will," Nancy promised. "Let's call my dad. Maybe he can help us."

They returned to the room and Nancy phoned Carson Drew. After she had filled him in on their adventure, she asked if he had heard from John Ford.

"No," he replied. "Not yet. But call me again tomorrow. Maybe he'll get in touch with me by then."

Next, Nancy called Mr. Watson. Midge's father, too, had bad news. He told the girls that he had not been offered the job and that he was returning to River Heights the next day.

As Midge was hanging up, there was a knock at the door. Nancy held her fingers to her lips as she went to open it.

"Who is it?" she called.

"Nina."

"Nina," Nancy cried, and let her friend in. "Are you all right? Has anything happened?"

Nina smiled. "Yes," she said. "Everything is fine at home. Uncle—I mean Mr. Calisher is completely changed."

Nancy motioned for the girl to sit down and then looked at her quizzically. "Completely changed?" she asked. "What do you mean?"

"I mean he's not nervous. He's not even nagging me about being scared of the threats. He told me the people making them were obviously bluffing and I should go ahead and play and not worry about anything."

Nancy stared at her friend. "That's strange."

"I know," Nina said. "And, of course, there

haven't been any more threats, since he was the one making them. What do you think it means, Nancy?"

Nancy tapped her lips with her forefinger. "I don't know. But I don't like it. I'll bet he's up to something. Don't lower your guard, Nina. And remember that the police are watching you. They probably followed you over here."

Nina nodded. "They did. There was a squad car about a block in back of me all the way."

"That makes me feel better," the girl detective declared. "How is Mrs. Calisher acting?"

"Well, she's calmed down, now that her husband isn't in a frenzy. I just wonder whether she knew all along what he was doing."

"Probably," Nancy said. "But we won't find out for sure until we clear up this whole thing."

"Will Aunt Emily have to go to prison, too, if he goes?" the young tennis player asked.

"Not if she wasn't actively involved in his scheme," Nancy replied.

"But wouldn't she be guilty of not reporting him?" Midge piped up.

"No," Nancy explained. "A wife does not have to testify against her husband."

"That's a relief," Nina said, getting up. "She's really a nice person. But she's afraid of him and does whatever he tells her. Well, I'd better get back."

The girls said good-bye with mutual promises to be in touch the next day. When Nina had left, Nancy sprawled in an easy chair and again went through all the details of the case. She did this frequently, assembling and reassembling in her mind the parts of the mystery, trying to figure out what she might have missed.

Then the phone rang. It was Carson Drew.

"Nancy, good news!" he said. "John Ford just called."

"Oh, that's wonderful, Dad!"

"What happened?" Midge squealed.

"Excuse me, Dad." Nancy turned to Midge. "John Ford called."

"Whoopee!" Midge shouted and turned a somersault on her bed.

"Tell me more, Dad." Nancy urged.

"Well," Carson Drew began, "I told him I would like to reopen his case, start appeal proceedings, and that you were looking for the safe."

"What did he say?"

"He was happy, of course, to know that we were trying so hard to help him, but he still refuses to turn himself in until that safe is recovered. However, he *is* willing to meet with me tomorrow in New Brighton. But he made me promise to do it on a strictly confidential basis. As his attorney, I can't violate our trust and tell the police. I hope that when I see him face to face I can persuade him."

Nancy bit her lip. "Well, good luck. We're trying hard here."

"I know you are, dear."

Nancy hung up.

"Nancy, there's one thing that bothers me," Midge said. "Why has Mr. Calisher suddenly relaxed and turned into a pussycat?"

"He's afraid we're on to him," Nancy replied. "When we exposed Ivan Foster, Mr. Calisher got scared and probably decided to lie low for a while—which makes it all the harder to get the goods on him." She sighed. "Well, we're not going to solve this puzzle tonight. Let's go to bed."

The next day at breakfast, Nancy suggested that they go down to the small lake that was near the motel.

"Why?" Midge asked.

"To clear our heads," Nancy grinned. Half an hour later, the young detectives were wandering along the shore, then Nancy sat on the grass. Midge idly built a little earth dam to block the stream that led into the lake while the older girl watched.

"Midge," Nancy suddenly cried. "Come on!" She got up and raced for the car.

"Wait!" Midge yelled, scrambling to her feet. "What's up?"

Nancy started the car as Midge jumped in next to her, then drove through the heavy traffic toward the River Heights Road.

"Remember the stream that ran across the road into a little pond on the right?" she asked. "Nothing was in the pond. But the crook could have dumped the safe right over the bridge into the mouth of the culvert. Probably he was able to push it in a little bit. The culvert is big enough. And with the slimy mud on the bottom, it would have slid in easy enough."

"Wow, you think so?"

"Yes, and I'll tell you why," the blond sleuth replied. "A blockage in the culvert would account for there only being the small trickle of water out the other side!"

"You're right!" Midge exclaimed. "Oh, let's hope it's the safe that's doing it!"

With their hearts beating fast, the girls drove quickly along the River Heights Road, this time to the second barricade, where Nancy carefully maneuvered around the obstacle and onto the blocked-off road.

When they reached the bridge over the stream, Nancy and Midge leaped out of the car and rushed to the pond. Intently, they peered into the culvert, but they could see nothing but a tangle of sticks, old weeds, and mud forming an effective dam.

"I'll look on the other side, Nancy," Midge offered. "Lend me your flashlight."

With the light in hand, Midge jumped down into the stream on the other side of the road. She disappeared into the culvert as Nancy peered into the gloom from above.

"See anything?" she called out.

There was no answer.

"Midge, do you see anything?"

"Watson," came the echoing reply. "I'm Watson."

Nancy smiled. "Okay. What do you see?"

Midge didn't answer. Instead, she just gave an incredible, joyous yell!

"Did you find it?" Nancy urged, her heart beating loudly.

"*I found it!*" Midge replied. "It's here! And it says Ford and Calisher right on the door, which is locked securely!"

"I found it! I found it!" Midge kept shouting over and over as she crawled out of the culvert pipe, wet and muddy and laughing with joy. Nancy, who had jumped down into the stream, grabbed her, heedless of the dirt. With their arms around each other, they danced and splashed in the six-inch stream.

When they stopped to catch their breath, they were both mud-spattered and soaked, but so happy they couldn't care less.

But suddenly they heard something that froze their blood. It was the sound of a car's engine straining and roaring, and of wheels spinning wildly. Someone was trying to drive around the first barricade!

19

A Bet Against Nancy

"I bet Ivan and Bull are behind us!" Midge cried. "They saw our tire marks from yesterday!"

Nancy was already bolting up the slope for the car. Midge followed and the two girls leaped in. Quickly Nancy started the engine.

"We have to lead them away from here and not let them suspect we found anything," she panted as she eased the blue sports sedan over the bridge.

"Nancy," Midge cried, staring back down the road, "you're going so slow. Hurry!"

"I'm just starting slow," the girl detective explained. "I don't want to show them that we stopped there and then took off fast by leaving a spin mark in the road."

Within a half mile, Midge reported the gray sedan in the distance, but Nancy easily made it to the main road before their pursuers could close the gap.

By the time the gray car was able to come within a hundred yards, the girls had reached the outskirts of New Brighton. Nancy felt sure the crooks would not try anything reckless in a built-up area, with people on the streets. She was right. The gray car hung back and eventually disappeared just before they came to police headquarters. But Nancy merely slowed down, then went past the police station to the New Brighton Motor Lodge. Midge looked at her inquiringly.

"I'll let Dad handle it," the young detective explained. "That safe contains his client's evidence and he should decide how to proceed from here on. He'll contact the police."

As soon as they reached the room, Nancy called her father, bubbling over with excitement. She gave him a complete report on where the safe was and about their pursuit by the crooks in the gray sedan. Carson Drew was elated.

"That's truly magnificent work, Nancy. I'm so proud of you and Midge!"

"Well, Dad," Nancy said, "you were the one who taught me to be persistent."

Carson Drew laughed. "I'm glad you listened. Well, let me go so I can call the police."

Nancy hung up, her eyes shining. "We did it!" she said. "Now it's up to Dad. Once they open that safe, John Ford should become a free man."

"That's great," Midge said. "Now let's tell Nina!"

Nancy dialed and heard Nina's strained voice.

"Are you all right?" the girl detective asked.

"Yes," the tennis star whispered, "but something's up. Mr. Calisher just left, and before that he and Aunt Emily whispered a lot. He was picked up by somebody in a black car."

"That's okay," Nancy said, "the police will tail him."

"There's something else," Nina added. "They've packed their bags and locked them in the bedroom closet. Nancy, I think they're getting ready to leave town."

"It does seem that way," Nancy admitted. "I'd better call Lieutenant Nelson and alert him."

Nancy reached the detective and relayed the information. "Is someone following Mr. Calisher?" she asked, when she had finished.

There was an embarrassed silence. "Ah, Nancy," the detective said, "I'm sorry, but we no longer have the black car under surveillance. We don't know where Aaron Calisher has gone."

"How could that happen?" Nancy asked, amazed.

"Our car had a blowout and by the time our man radioed for another car, we'd lost Calisher. But we'll be looking for him."

Nancy thanked him, hung up, then dialed Nina again. "Nina," she said, "do you have any idea where Mr. Calisher went?"

"I don't know for sure. He has been picked up by that black car several times before, and once I heard him tell Aunt Emily that he was going to Foxhall."

"What's Foxhall?" Nancy asked.

"A big mansion on the North Hudson Highway near the intersection of Indian Road. Are you going out there, Nancy?"

"Yes. The police can't go in there without a warrant, and right now that'll take time. Meanwhile, if I have to do a little trespassing to prove Aaron Calisher is guilty, I will."

"Oh, Nancy, be careful!"

"Don't worry. But now for the really important news, Nina. We found the safe!"

Nina gasped, then shouted in delight, "Oh, Nancy, I can't believe it!"

"And your father is meeting with my dad today. With the evidence, he should be free tomorrow."

Nancy hung up, leaving Nina deliriously happy. But Nancy now had her mind on the mysterious Foxhall Mansion. Then she checked over her emergency gear, some of which was in the car trunk. "We need a flashlight, climbing rope, grappling hook, tape recorder with new batteries, and a tear gas defense capsule—that's about it," she said, as Midge looked at her curiously. "—And comfortable clothes."

The girls dressed in sweat pants and sweaters. Nancy outfitted Midge from her own wardrobe, rolling up sleeves and pantlegs; then they started out for Foxhall Mansion.

Nancy drove as swiftly as possible, since Aaron Calisher already had more than a half hour start. Fortunately, she found the Tudor mansion without difficulty. A black sedan stood in the driveway. Nancy parked under a clump of concealing trees, some distance down the road.

"This is fun," whispered Midge as they approached the metal fence that surrounded the property.

"Yes," Nancy said, "as long as the fence isn't

electrified, and there aren't any guard dogs inside—or armed guards. And," she added, "if we can actually get into the place and find out what Calisher is doing. For all we know, he may just be attending a club meeting."

"Do you really think so?" asked Midge, disappointed.

"No," Nancy chuckled. "I just want to let you know the odds against us. Now let's try the final test."

Nancy picked a quarter out of her pocket and lobbed it at the fence. It bounced off harmlessly, without sparks, and proved that the fence was not electrified. Quickly, the girls climbed over and dropped down on the grass inside.

It was getting dark, but still the girls hid behind a tree for a full five minutes, prepared to flee at the sight or sound of guard dogs, but there were none. Finally Nancy motioned to Midge and, in a deep crouch, they moved the fifty feet to the mansion.

They found themselves under a row of heavy, leaded windows at ground level that had been left open. There were no lights on in the room and, after a careful look, Nancy boosted herself up and through the window. Midge followed.

Cautiously they moved through the house

until they saw a light under a door and heard the sound of voices. "Calisher is in there," Nancy whispered, picking his voice out of the crowd. "We have to get close enough to tape him."

But how? The big double doors could not be opened without alerting the men on the inside. Nancy's eyes swept over the hallway in which they were standing. There were doors on either side of the room that Calisher was in. Perhaps one of them would lead to an adjoining entrance!

The girls tiptoed to the one on the right to go in when suddenly the door was thrown open!

Instantly, the young detectives flattened themselves against the wall. For the moment, the door concealed them from the man who opened it. He was a butler carrying a tray of dirty glasses! Nancy held her breath as the man kicked the door shut behind him and, without looking back, walked down the hall and disappeared into what was evidently the kitchen.

"This is the right way," Nancy whispered. "He just came out of that room by another entrance!"

Quickly the girls slipped through the door and found themselves in an L-shaped room. They dropped to their knees behind a huge stuffed chair and saw a group of men talking around a coffee table at the far end.

Their voices were more distinct now but Nancy still needed to get closer. Signaling Midge, she crawled along the back of a large sofa to a drapery covering one complete wall.

The girls inched their way to a spot barely six feet from Calisher. He was talking with a tall, well-dressed man with dark hair and eyes. The man wore a huge diamond ring and in back of him stood two big, ugly men, obviously his bodyguards. Behind Calisher, sitting on a long, low couch, were Ivan Foster and Bull Tolliver. Nancy switched on the tape recorder.

"So here it is. We've been stopped because of this confounded Nancy Drew. She's gotten in our way every time," Calisher was saying.

"Right," the smooth, dark man said coldly. "Three times we've trusted you to handle things and three times you've messed up. I lost a lot of money on those bets. I don't like to lose money, Calisher. If I lose tomorrow, something very unpleasant is going to happen to you."

Nancy and Midge, who were crouched down and peeking under the drape, could see Calisher turn white.

"Now, Silk," he whined, "that's not fair. I've also bet a lot of money! You know I'm going to sell the business to cover my gambling debts to you, and *I'm* betting on tomorrow's match, too."

Silk scowled at him.

"Give me a break," pleaded Calisher.

"You'll get a break," Silk hissed. "My boys here are good at breaking things and if you don't guarantee results this time, they're going to start working on you!"

"Don't worry, Silk," squeaked Calisher, mopping his brow. "I've got a surefire way of handling Nina and her snoopy friends."

Nancy felt Midge stir and instantly nudged her to be still.

"Yeah," Silk said, "and how's that?"

"Nina will sleep right through the game," Calisher replied. "As for Nancy Drew— well—my boys are going to take care of her." He pointed at Ivan and Bull. "She just might have an accident."

Nancy and Midge tensed when they heard Aaron Calisher's threat, and any sympathy they might have had for the man's predicament vanished.

"I'll believe it when I see it, Calisher," Silk said after a moment's pause. "You have a way of ruining the simplest operation. And I wouldn't trust those two stupid goons of yours to carry out my garbage."

Ivan Foster and Bull Tolliver glared furiously but said nothing as they eyed the bulges under the coats of Silk's bodyguards. They knew the bulges most likely were weapons.

"You never did find that safe, did you?" Silk growled at them. "You all got a lot to lose if that kid detective finds it before you do. You'll all wind up in prison. Now get out of here. You," pointing to one of his guards, "drive these people back where you got them."

Aaron Calisher stood up, trembling, "Come on, men, let's go." He hurried out of the house with his scowling henchmen and Silk's driver following him.

Moments later, Silk and the remaining bodyguard left the room, and Nancy and Midge were alone. "Did you tape all that, Nancy?"

"Yes," said Nancy. "At least I hope I got it all. Now we have to get this tape to the police and stop Calisher from doing whatever he's planning to do to Nina. Did you hear him say, 'She'll sleep right through the match'?"

"Yes," Midge said. "I'll bet he's going to drug her."

Nancy nodded. "He's a desperate man. Come on, let's hurry."

The girls inched their way down the wall inside the protection of the drapery until they

came to a window. Nancy swung it open and slipped out. Midge followed and they ran swiftly away from the house. But as they were about to climb the fence they heard a shout. "Stop! Trespassers!"

"Up you go. Hurry!" Nancy cried, and boosted Midge up to the fence. Then she followed in an instant. When she reached the top, she saw the bodyguard and Silk galloping across the lawn.

Nancy jumped to the other side of the fence, hit the ground with a thud, and rolled like a paratrooper to lessen the shock of the impact.

"Hurry!" called Midge, who was twenty feet ahead and looking back. Nancy started to run, then suddenly stopped. She realized she had dropped the tape recorder! The two thugs had rushed up to the fence, then turned to run for the gate, which was fifty feet away.

Desperately, Nancy began to look in the thick tall grass behind her, trying to find the recorder. "Nancy!" she heard Midge shout. "What are you waiting for?"

20

Sweep to Victory

The girl detective had just about decided to leave the recorder and run, when her foot kicked against it. Relieved, she reached down and scooped it up, then dashed after Midge.

Behind her came the pounding of feet. She felt confident that she could outrun the heavy-footed bodyguard—but could she get the car started in time? When she was less than one hundred feet away, she heard the engine roar to life and saw Midge make a U-turn so the car would be headed in the right direction. All Nancy had to do was leap in!

A moment later, they left the fuming, shouting thugs in the driveway. "See," Midge said. "Aren't you glad I can drive a car?"

"Am I ever," Nancy cried, exhaling in relief.

"But now I'd better get behind the wheel again." The girls changed places and Nancy drove straight back to the motel, which was closer than the Calishers' house. Nancy quickly dialed Nina from the lobby. Luckily, the girl answered the telephone. "Nina, don't eat or drink *anything*," she said. "You may be drugged. I'll be over as soon as I can!"

"Okay," Nina replied. "I'll go next door to the Fishers' until you come. It's the gray house with black shutters."

"Good idea." Nancy hung up, then rang the police. She outlined the plan and asked them to send a plainclothesman in an unmarked car to the house next door, which they agreed to do.

Then the girls went to the desk to see if there were any messages. They found out Mr. Drew had arrived and was waiting for them. Happily they ran to his room and knocked.

"Welcome ladies," the lawyer said. "Have you had an interesting afternoon?"

"Oh, Daddy, how did you guess?" Nancy said, kissing him. Carson Drew had ordered sodas and the thirsty girls helped themselves and then sat down to trade information.

Mr. Drew reported he had led the police to the safe and it had been recovered and opened.

"And?" Nancy asked eagerly, "were the papers there? Did they prove Mr. Ford's innocence? Did Mr. Ford surrender? Is he free on a bond?"

"Wait, wait," her father said, smiling. "There's a small hitch."

"What is it, Dad?" Nancy urged.

"Water got into the safe and the documents were damaged. They're being dried out. We won't know till morning whether we can read them."

Nancy bit her lip. "You'll *have* to be able to read them!" she insisted. "Now, look what *I* have. A tape recording of Calisher and a gambler named Silk talking about their scheme to fix the tennis matches!"

"What!" the lawyer exclaimed. "Let's hear it!"

He rewound the tape, then pushed the start button, and they all listened eagerly. But as they did, Mr. Drew frowned, and Nancy's face also showed dismay.

Midge looked at them. "What's the matter?"

"It's worthless, isn't it, Dad?" Nancy said.

Carson Drew nodded. "I'm afraid so. They did a lot of talking but they didn't say a single thing that really incriminates them. There's no way you can use this as solid evidence to convict them. Not once do they say they're fixing the matches or threatening Nina. All Calisher says is that she won't make the match because she'll sleep through it."

Nancy got up and paced the floor. "Oh, Dad, this is frustrating. We all know what he means. He's going to do something to make Nina sleep. But what? Put sleeping pills in her food or drink?"

"Possibly," Mr. Drew said. "Or worse."

Nancy sat down, deep in thought. Nina had mentioned that Calisher had packed his bags. This meant he was preparing to flee the town, perhaps flee the country. He was just waiting to collect on his bet. He would not leave until the match was over. But what was he planning to do to Nina? The only way to trap him on the charge of fixing the tennis match was to let him make his move. If the police intervened now, he would be tipped off—and still no evidence.

According to Silk, the documents in the safe were enough to convict Calisher, probably of the same mail fraud that had implicated Mr. Ford. But suppose the documents were not legible when they were dried out?

Nancy jumped up. "Well, I can't do anything about the contents of the safe, Dad. That's in your hands. But I can try to save Nina. I'm going to go over there right now."

"Good luck," said her father. "And both of

you please be careful."

Nancy and Midge started off for the Calishers' street. They pulled up in front of a gray, Victorian-style house, and Nina waved from the wide porch. Then she came down the steps, and together the girls walked next door.

"Mr. Calisher and Aunt Emily went out," Nina reported as they joined the policeman, who had gotten out of his unmarked car. Mr. Calisher got back just after you called, Nancy, and as soon as I told them I was going next door, they left."

"That must have been before I arrived," the detective said. "No one has come or gone since I got here."

Nancy made a face. "I sure hope they didn't disappear for good," she said. "Let's go upstairs and check the closet."

On the way to the second floor, Nina asked Nancy how she knew that Mr. Calisher might have planned to drug her, and Nancy told her what she had overheard at Foxhall Mansion.

When the group arrived in the bedroom, the closet door was open.

"The bags are gone!" Nina cried out.

"Oh, no!" Nancy said. "They must have been afraid that we were on to them, so they left. But it seems to me Mr. Calisher wouldn't just give up on the tennis match. He needs that money or

Silk's men will get rough with him."

"But how can he do anything to Nina if he isn't here?" Midge asked.

"I don't know," Nancy said.

The policeman shrugged. "Well, I have instructions to guard you, Nina. I'd better get down and watch the house. If you need me, you know where I am." With that, he went back to his post.

"It's strange the Calishers left like that, without even writing me a note," Nina said thoughtfully.

"I know," Nancy admitted. "I just can't believe he would take off without the money he stands to make. Why don't we just wait and see if we hear from them tonight."

"Meanwhile, could we get something to eat?" Midge piped up. "I'm starved!"

Nina laughed. "Let's raid the refrigerator."

The girls went into the kitchen and Nina opened the refrigerator door. Suddenly she cried out in surprise. "Here's a note. This is where they left it!" she said.

"Note?" Nancy asked. "Let me see it."

Nina took a bottle with a piece of paper attached to it out of the refrigerator. "This is my special protein drink," she explained. "It's made with milk, juices, vitamins and minerals. It's my coach's recipe and I have it every night and early in the morning before a match."

She took the message off the bottle and handed it to Nancy, who unfolded it and read aloud:

> *"Dear Nina: Aunt Emily and I will be out late tonight, so please don't wait up for us. But be sure to drink your energy booster.*
>
> *"Love, Uncle Aaron."*

Nancy looked up in time to see Nina uncap the bottle and lift it to her lips. "Nina! Don't drink that!" she cried out.

Nina jumped. "Oh, I almost forgot!"

Nancy took the bottle. "I'll bet he put a strong sleeping potion in here. If you drink it, you'll probably be out for twenty-four hours."

"Are you sure, Nancy?" Nina asked.

"No. But we can't take any chances. We'll have the drink analyzed. Also, Midge and I will stay with you tonight in case the Calishers come back."

Nancy went to call her father, who promised to have a policeman pick up the bottle to take to the lab.

"Good," Nancy said. "Oh, and Dad?"

"Yes?"

"Could you ask him to bring over some hamburgers? There wasn't much in the refrigerator."

Mr. Drew laughed. "Consider it done."

Half an hour later, a young detecive arrived with a bag of hamburgers and soda. He took the bottle and drove straight to the police laboratory with it, while the girls hungrily devoured the food.

The next morning, the girls were awakened by the telephone ringing. It was Mr. Drew. "Great news, Nancy," he reported. "The booster bottle Calisher left for Nina contained enough sleeping potion to keep her in dreamland for a whole day. And the documents are dry *and* readable. Mr. Ford will be free after the formalities are taken care of, which shouldn't take long. I'm sure I can speed things up."

"Wonderful!" Nancy cried out.

"If you bring Nina down to headquarters, she can have a reunion with her father before the match. John is here now."

"We'll be right there!" Nancy said.

"Oh, one more thing," Mr. Drew added. "We've recalled your guard. You won't need him any longer, and he's going to follow you over here."

Nancy rushed to tell Nina the news, and ten minutes later the three girls were on their way to police headquarters. Tears of joy ran down Nina's cheeks when she saw her father, and the two embraced. "Oh, Father, you're free—*free!* It's as if a nightmare has turned into a dream," his daughter sobbed in his arms.

Finally Mr. Drew spoke up. "Nina, I hate to rush you, but you'll have to get to your game. Your dad can come with you; he's been released even though we haven't finished the paperwork."

"What about the Calishers?" Nancy inquired. "They didn't come home last night."

"The police have sealed all roads and the airport," Mr. Drew said. "They won't get away. Now why don't you and Midge run along and watch Nina win."

"I hope she does," Midge spoke up. "It's Friday the thirteenth today. I'm not sure that's good."

"Oh," Nancy exclaimed. "I almost forgot! That means I can still make it to the bicentennial rehearsal tomorrow!"

Nancy phoned the bicentennial office and spoke to the delighted Mrs. Milton. Then she and Midge headed to the tennis club and took seats next to the beaming Mr. Ford.

Nina was so happy that she played better than she ever had before and swept to victory over her talented opponent in straight sets.

After the game, Nancy and Midge went to the locker room to say good-bye to the young tennis star. Nina hugged them both. "Oh, Nancy, if it hadn't been for you and Midge, there'd be no victories at all."

"Watson," Midge murmured.

Nina kissed her on the cheek. "Watson—Nancy—we'll stay in close touch. You'll always be my very best friends!"

The girls and Mr. Ford parted with the promise to see each other again soon. Then Midge and Nancy headed for their car.

"Hey," Midge said suddenly, "Shouldn't you call Bess and tell her you'll be able to make the rehearsal? She must be having a giant fit by now."

Nancy laughed. "You're so right."

They headed for a pay phone, and Nancy rang the Marvin house. When Bess came on the line, she exploded with joy. "I've heard from Mrs. Milton!" she cried. "And you know what? Kimberly's mother just called. Kim's in bed with a bad headache. Oh, I'm so tempted to send her a bouquet of sour grapes. Just hurry home, Nancy."

Nancy and Midge arrived in River Heights in time for dinner that night. Midge received permission from her father to sleep at Nancy's house and was preparing to leave with her friend for rehearsal the next day when Mr. Drew pulled into the driveway.

"I have lots of news!" he announced to the two girls. "First of all, John Ford won't have to go through another trial. He is planning to resume running his business and to persuade Sam Jackson to work for him."

"Oh, that's wonderful!" Nancy cried.

"Yes, it is," Mr. Drew agreed. "Now, are you ready for the next part? The Calishers were arrested at the airport shortly after the match, and Bull Tolliver and Ivan Foster were caught after trying to smash through a police roadblock. A thirteen-state alarm has been issued for the notorious Mr. Silk, which will make it impossible for him to hide very long."

"Did Mr. Calisher confess?" Midge asked. She was beaming with excitement.

"Yes. He has admitted not only the mail fraud and the attempts to fix the tennis matches, but also the framing of his partner, Ford, so he would wind up with all the assets of the business. He had enormous gambling debts and was under pressure from Silk to repay the money. When he overheard Nina on the phone asking Nancy to help her find out who was threatening her, he became very upset. He had Ivan Foster tail Nancy to scare her away—but, of course, it didn't work."

"What about Mrs. Calisher?" Nancy inquired.

"She was absolved of any direct guilt. Calisher said she didn't know about his criminal activities, and there was no evidence to hold her. As Nina knows, she was basically a good person who only knew her husband as an unfortunate gambler. She'll live with her sister from now on and let time help her straighten out her life."

"Well then," Nancy said with a big smile, "everything is back to normal." Secretly, the girl detective wondered how long things would stay that way. She had no idea that soon she would encounter *The Mysterious Image*.

At that moment, the front door burst open and Bess Marvin rushed in. She skidded to a stop in front of her friend. "Nancy, take my pulse. Kimberly just called the office. She's made a miraculous recovery and *will* be on the float as runner-up. But now she wants the ladies-in-waiting not only to curtsy, but to blow *kisses*, and—get this—to both *her and you*. She even put herself first!"

Nancy, Midge, and Carson Drew broke into laughter. "As I said," Nancy giggled. "Everything's back to normal!"